A CHIMAERA IN
MY WARDROBE

A CHIMAERA IN MY WARDROBE

Tina Rath

CHIVERS

British Library Cataloguing in Publication Data available

This Large Print edition published by AudioGO Ltd, Bath, 2013.

Published by arrangement with the Author

U.K.   Hardcover   ISBN   978 1 4713 4129 8
U.K.   Softcover   ISBN   978 1 4713 4130 4

Printed and bound in Great Britain by
TJ International Ltd

CONTENTS

THE FIRST STORY

I found the chimaera hiding in a corner of my wardrobe one evening in early summer.

I was doing free-lance work as an SA ('supporting artiste') and model, and selling the odd short story to support myself while I wrote my novel. My One True Love was back-packing around the world with a video camera, in a belated gap-year, with the idea that he would, on his return, find a job, while editing his travel footage into something marketable. And then we would set up house together and live happily ever after.

I had just been told to present myself at a certain film location at seven o'clock the next morning, with three completely different outfits: smart/casual, business like and 'funky'. No one at my agency was able to explain quite what 'funky' meant, so I decided to interpret it as 'peculiar' and I mounted an expedition into the far reaches of my wardrobe to find something odd enough.

And instead I found the chimaera.

I knew it was a chimaera because it had a lion's head, a goat's body and a serpent's tail, just as the Classical Dictionary describes it. It was quite a small monster. The lion's head was not much bigger than a good-sized cat, although the mane, of course, made it look larger. The goat's body included the forelegs, but there were no back legs: the body tapered off into a scaly snake's tail. That bit looked rather like the pictures you sometimes see of Capricorn, with a goat's body and fishy tail. It had managed to fold itself into quite a small space, where it huddled, looking rather pathetic and more than a little transparent. I supposed it must have originated on some film set or casting studio, forming out of the broken dreams and strange imaginings that infest such places and frequently coalesce into even weirder forms. Somehow, at the end of a busy day I must have gathered it up and packed it with my clothes, tarot cards, paperback, embroidery, notebook and mobile phone and brought it home without noticing. I might have left it in peace in my wardrobe, but I fancied that it was exuding a faint, cloudy dampness, which would do my clothes no good. I went to the kitchen, and found some stale sponge fingers, and broke them up to make a trail from the wardrobe to my sitting room, hoping that hunger might induce it to follow them.

Sure enough, I had hardly packed everything for the next day in my bag, when I heard a faint crunching sound, and the chimaera came softly into the room, nibbling and nosing delicately at the biscuits. It seemed to manage its goat's legs and snake's tail quite easily, balancing on its front hooves, and carrying the tail in a coil over its back like a scorpion. I offered it a small saucer of herb tea, and it lapped a little, gratefully, I thought. Its tongue was the soft clean pink of a kitten's. The sponge fingers and the tea had helped to firm it up a little, and it began to look quite solid. You could now see what colour it was. The lion part was a very light blonde which blended seamlessly into a white goat bit, the hooves were pink, and the tail had nacreous pink and golden scales. Its eyes were just that shade of that deep red amber which is called 'cherry colour' and the pupils were not slit, like an animal's, but round and human. It was really quite attractive, even if you were queasy about snakes. When it had finished the tea it turned its little lion head towards me and said, 'Thank you,' in a small, breathy voice.

I jumped slightly, spilling some of my tea. 'I didn't know that chimaeras could talk,' I said.

'Oh, yes,' it replied, 'I think you'll find that all we fabulous monsters are quite good conversationalists. Look at the sphinx.'

I remembered that the sphinx could not only speak, but was quite famous for asking rather clever riddles. Of course it then strangled or ate the people who couldn't answer them, but the chimaera did not seem at all fierce or dangerous. Indeed I felt I should apologise for forgetting that monsters could speak but it politely waved my apology aside with a delicate front hoof. It told me that it had indeed come from some film-set but it could not remember

3

which. It was quite happy in my wardrobe, but it would be happier still if I would permit it to use my sitting room at such times as I was not using it myself. I did not like to ask how long it intended to stay, but perhaps it could read my thoughts, as it assured me that it would probably not last the summer. It would either dissipate, 'quite painlessly,' as it reassured me, or, perhaps mutate into a more socially acceptable shape.

I was quite happy to allow it to use the sitting room. It seemed a gentle, rather companionable creature, with a great deal of quiet charm, but I did wonder about its dietary requirements. Its teeth, although small, and pearly, looked rather sharp. Again, it reassured me before I could ask. As a mythological creature, it said, it could live— indeed preferred to live—on cloud vapour and honey dew (although the sponge biscuits had been very welcome)—the first was readily available from my sitting-room window (I lived, at the time, in a very high attic), and the latter, in the form of diluted honey, I undertook to supply.

'I would, of course, like to pay some rent,' said the chimaera when we had settled that it need only retire to the wardrobe when I had visitors. I assured it that rent would not be necessary, but curiosity drove me to inquire about the currency it had in mind.

'I could tell you stories,' said the chimaera.

'If you like.'

I agreed that I liked stories very much, but I felt sure that I had heard quite enough of the kind of stories you might hear around film sets and casting studios.

'Oh, no. My tales are very different and original. Would you like to hear one now?'

Common politeness demanded that I say yes. And the chimaera began to speak, not in the strange, breathless little voice it had used in conversation, but with clear, assured tones—I was never quite sure if it was a male or a female voice, but it was a very pleasant and soothing one, just right for a story-teller.

The first story it told me, that evening was the strange tale of:

THE INCIDENT IN RAMILLIES GARDENS

'Is anyone near Ramillies Gardens?' inquired the radio. 'We have a report of a disturbance.'

'What kind of disturbance?' said Sergeant Prendergast through a mouthful of chips. 'Not a Domestic, is it?'

'You don't get Domestics in places like Ramillies Gardens, Sarge,' said PC Oliver, shocked. 'They're all accountants and company directors up there.'

'Accountants can have rows like anyone

else,' said the Sergeant, heavily. 'You get an accountant coming at you with a poker and he's as dangerous as a coal heaver. And it's a full moon tonight. Makes people violent.'

'Now, psychiatrists have exploded that theory . . .' PC Oliver began, but the Sergeant brushed that aside.

'A few years' experience on the beat will tell you more about loonies than all those trick-cyclists can.'

He was clearly about to give the young PC the benefit of that experience, although as far as the young Oliver could see, his Sergeant's life had been spent in the single-minded pursuit of carbohydrate, chiefly in the shape of chips and pies, and of cups of tea, very hot, very strong 'and two sugars, if you don't mind, dear' combined with strict avoidance of Domestics, so he was not sorry when the radio interrupted them again. 'Look, is anyone in the vicinity of Ramillies Gardens?' it inquired plaintively.

'Is it urgent?' said Sergeant Prendergast.

'Yes,' said the radio, firmly. 'A Mrs Fortescue has reported a dangerous wild animal in her back garden.'

'Ah. That'll be cats,' said Sergeant Prendergast.

'Dangerous wild cats?' PC Oliver queried hopefully.

'No, just noisy ones. Some old biddy has been woken up by some naughty pussies courting in the privet, and she has naturally called in the law.'

'Is anyone going to deal with this?' the radio demanded.

'Yeah, we might as well go along,' said the Sergeant cheerfully. 'We'll throw some water over the bad marauding moggies, and make the world safe for the residents of Ramillies Gardens. And Ma Fortescue can make us a cup of cha.'

'Let's burn rubber,' said PC Oliver. He was young, and had not yet lost his enthusiasm. 'Shall I sound the siren?'

'No, lad, we don't want to *warn* the moggies, now do we?'

But when they arrived at the scene of the disturbance they discovered it was rather more serious than stray cats. It was certainly bigger. They surveyed it cautiously from Mrs Fortescue's kitchen window, as it ranged round and round her miniscule back garden.

'It's a stag, Sarge,' breathed PC Oliver, 'it's a socking great stag—look at those horns . . .'

'Antlers, lad, antlers,' said his mentor.

The light from the kitchen window glittered on a thicket of wicked points as the beast threw back its head and roared aloud. Lights went on in several neighbouring houses.

'I never knew they made a noise like that,' said PC Oliver unhappily.

'They don't all talk English with cute American accents, like a lot of little Bambis,'

Prendergast told him.

'But where did it come from?'

Unexpectedly Mrs Fortescue had an answer to that.

'Next door's garden,' she said, 'look, you can see where it tramped down the fence to get in here. Who's going to pay for that, that's what I'd like to know?'

'Well, you're insured, aren't you missus?' said Prendergast unsympathetically. Mrs Fortescue had shown no sign of reaching for the teapot.

'Not against stags I'm not. They'll probably say it's an act of God. Now, what are you going to do about it?'

'I don't see what we can do,' said Prendergast. 'You don't expect us to arrest it, do you? I don't know why you didn't call the RSPCA.'

'I did,' she said shortly. 'They told me to call you.' Her tone suggested that she thought very little of this advice.

'Perhaps we could contact some kind of specialist organisation with experience of stags,' said PC Oliver. 'I mean, I know there's an Owl Protection League. My aunt found an injured owl outside a pub once—well she thought it was a paper bag, but . . .'

'And you think these Owl people might be able to deal with a mad stag? I mean, they're not very similar.'

'No, Sarge, but there might be a Deer

Protection League who'd have the right sort of equipment to handle it. They sent someone to collect my aunt's owl with gloves, and a big cage.'

'You'll need more than gloves to catch that, lad,' Sergeant Prendergast said grimly, watching the beast plunge past the window again.

'It's ruining my antirrhinums,' said Mrs Fortescue. 'Why can't it stay on the path?'

'It looks—sort of—uncoordinated to me,' said PC Oliver suddenly. 'It's staggering a bit. I reckon it's not too well, Sarge.'

They watched carefully. The stag certainly seemed to be having problems with co-ordinating all four of its hooves at once.

'Do stags get hydrophobia?' PC Oliver asked nervously.

'It doesn't seem to be foaming at the mouth—still perhaps we should radio for a police marksman. Better safe than sorry.'

'You don't mean you're going to shoot him!' Mrs Fortescue exclaimed. She flung herself in front of the window. 'Over my dead body!'

'I thought you wanted to get rid of it,' Sergeant Prendergast protested. 'Wasn't that why you called us in?'

'I want it out of my back garden, but I'm not going to stand by and watch it murdered in cold blood.'

'Could it—er—belong to your neighbour?' PC Oliver asked, hopefully. 'As it's come from her garden. Perhaps she might know what to do about it.'

'Well, unless she's been hiding it in the garden shed . . .' Sergeant Prendergast began, but he started to move towards the door. It was always possible that Mrs Fortescue's neighbour might be more forthcoming with the tea.

By mutual consent they made no attempt to go through Mrs Fortescue's back garden. They went out of her front door, and Sergeant Prendergast lumbered down her path, and up the neighbouring one, while PC Oliver lightly hurdled the low wall dividing the gardens, and rang the doorbell. The door was opened immediately by a tall and very beautiful young woman who was wearing a plain dark dressing gown firmly fastened right up to her white throat. She had a mass of silvery blonde hair that was also firmly fastened round her head, although numberless fine filaments had escaped, giving her a luminous halo as she stood outlined against the light.

'No need for alarm, Miss,' said PC Oliver. 'But we've had a report of a wild animal . . .'

'Yes?' said the young woman, opening her large, silvery blue eyes.

PC Oliver found his throat had suddenly gone dry. He was grateful when Sergeant Prendergast joined them.

'Your—er—neighbour suggested that it might have come from your garden.'

She raised her finely arched brows. 'Why?'

'I take it you heard the disturbance, Miss,' said Sergeant Prendergast.

'I heard the poor creature bellowing,' she allowed. 'Have you contacted Lord Cravenham?'

Two dropped jaws told her that they had not.

'He has converted his estate into a theme park which includes *The Robin Hood Experience*. I suppose the creature could have escaped from there.'

Mrs Fortescue, who had followed the policeman up the path, was already obtaining Lord Cravenham's number from directory enquiries on her mobile. She had contacted his lordship before Sergeant Prendergast could co-opt the idea for himself. 'He's sending a van,' she announced triumphantly.

'Good,' said Sergeant Prendergast. 'We'll wait for that van in your kitchen, if we may. Perhaps you could get the kettle on . . .' he noticed that his colleague was staring past the younger woman's shoulder, as if he saw something strange about her patio doors, which were visible at the far end of her sitting-room. 'Come along, Oliver.'

The man from Lord Cravenham's deer-park eventually arrived. He was wearing a bright green costume, suggestive of Peter Pan rather than Robin Hood, but apart from that he seemed competent enough. The stag had calmed down considerably while the two policemen were drinking their tea, and it allowed itself to be caught quite easily. But then they were faced with a problem. There was only one way to leave the garden, and that was through the house. Mrs Fortescue's house was as its Victorian builders had left it, and the beast would have to negotiate kitchen, sitting room and hall. Her young neighbour, on the other hand, had what estate agents call a through lounge, one large room giving a comparatively easy passage from garden to street.

Sergeant Prendergast knocked on her patio doors and the young woman, still wrapped tightly in her dressing gown, opened them. She cut through the men's explanations, and stood aside so that they could lead the creature through her sitting room.

'Is this yours?' PC Oliver asked, picking up a canvas bag that was lying in a flowerbed. He took a look at the contents and frowned. 'You shouldn't leave tools outside at night you know—a burglar could . . .' he was cut off by a sharp kick on the ankle from his superior officer.

'No problem at all,' said the Sergeant, scooping up the bag, 'Miss—er—'

'Mooney,' said the young lady.

'Yes. Indeed. Mooney,' he repeated. An Irish name, PC Oliver thought, and wondered, suddenly, if she could ever have been a nun.

There was something rather austere and nun-like about her, in spite of that mass of blonde hair. And the fact that even that dressing gown could not hide the outlines of a body that looked like some delicious amalgamation of super-model and Olympic athlete. Then he pulled himself together, and followed his Sergeant. Two policeman, a deer warden and a stag made their way carefully out to the street.

They watched the deer loaded into the van, and went to their own car.

'Sarge,' said PC Oliver, nervously.

'Yes, lad?'

'Someone has tried to break into Miss Mooney's house. There were marks on those patio doors. And that bag—I could swear I've seen it before. It belongs to Arnie Taylor.'

'Yes, lad. Arnie Taylor the burglar.'

'So what the hell's been going on?'

'I think Miss—er—Mooney was woken up by the noise of Arnie Taylor trying to break in through those patio doors. He always was clumsy. And, rashly perhaps, she ran downstairs to see what was going on . . .' he hesitated.

'Yes—and then he was scared off by the stag. But where did the stag come from?'

'No, lad, he wasn't scared by the stag. I think Miss Mooney sleeps in the all-together, and she didn't wait to put on her dressing gown. So Arnie Taylor saw her starkers. And he turned into the stag.'

PC Oliver tried, unobtrusively, to edge away. His colleague had clearly gone very mad indeed.

'You see,' the Sergeant continued serenely, 'she's an avatar of the moon goddess, Diana, or Artemis, depending on whether you prefer the Latin or the Greek. The virgin huntress. The name's a dead give-away, never mind the looks. She shines in the dark, as you probably didn't notice when she stepped into the garden. Of course, it's happened at least once before. A chap called Actaeon came across her when she was swimming in the nuddy. Same thing. Turned into a stag. Didn't they teach you these things at school?'

The chimaera fell silent.

'What happened to the stag?' I asked.

'It lived in Lord Cravenham's deer-park until the next full moon, and then it changed back into Arnie Taylor. He was much luckier than Actaeon, who was torn to pieces by his own hounds. Arnie had lost his nerve, and he was unable to pursue his career as a burglar so he joined Lord Cravenham's staff in the theme park. After all, he could say that he really knew about deer, from the inside, as it were. The worst effect of his experience was that he was that he developed a severe allergy to redcurrant sauce.'

THE SECOND STORY

The next day after I discovered the chimaera I had to leave very early in the morning, and I did not see it before I went. I supposed it was curled up asleep in my wardrobe, and I envied it a little as I made my way through the dawn-lit streets to catch the first tube of the day. But I quickly forgot about it in the hurry of getting to my destination, and passing the ordeal of inspection by Wardrobe. This is always performed by a very young girl, clutching a clipboard. I suspect they have been specially trained to look you up and down, from head to foot, and then say, with a tiny sigh 'Did you bring anything else?'—after which they turn down all your alternative out-fits and grudgingly allow that you might as well keep on what you have. Sometimes even this will not do, and the young person will say 'Have we got *anything* that might fit this lady?' and a very humiliating procedure will follow while they try to find something.

This particular Wardrobe was especially scathing about my attempts to be 'funky' for which I could hardly blame her. Although I did feel that her final choice, which consisted of my 'business-like' jacket with the 'funky' skirt was perhaps a serious mistake and may have explained why I was not allowed within twenty

15

five feet of the camera for the entire day.

However, I did not really mind. The shoot was in the grounds of a rather grand house, and we extras could sit in the gardens in the sunshine drinking coffee, when we were not required on set, which, in my case was all the time, although once or twice I was sent along by a hopeful AD and very promptly sent back again, by the Director. When everyone had finished their newspapers, we passed the time by seeing how many card games could be played using a tarot deck. Snap was difficult, Happy Families not impossible, but a rather complicated form of poker, using all the major arcana proved the most entertaining. And at the end of the day, I was asked to return 'for continuity'. I could not even imagine why I had actually to be present to ensure a continuous non-appearance, but I was not about to argue. It was, after all, another day's work.

But I returned home late in the evening, a prey to a certain mild anxiety. I had remembered, as I sat waiting for a train that chimaeras were, according to *The Classical Dictionary*, fire-breathing monsters, and I wondered if I might return to find my home in ashes and if the insurance would refuse to pay out on the grounds that I had—illegally—sublet my wardrobe to a chimaera.

But all was well. Indeed the faintly cool damp atmosphere that my particular chimaera seemed to exhale made my sitting room feel rather pleasant than otherwise, after a long hot day. The only other sign of its presence were some curious glittering webs, as fine as spider silk, but shot with bright colours that hovered in the air above the sofa. It told me that it had spent much of its day dreaming and these webs were the remnants of its dreams. As the dusk grew in the room the webs glowed more brightly, then vanished in a scattering of tiny cool sparks.

I had a shower, put on a clean light cotton dress, and made a pot of herb tea, which I took into the sitting room. I had opened the window a little, so that the chimaera might refresh itself by lapping alternately at the faintly crimson clouds of evening, and a small saucer of honey, and when it had finished its supper we sat and talked, and drank herb tea. The chimaera, having its origin on a film-set, knew all the technical terms, and it was rather pleasant to discuss the minor events of my day with a creature who did not need to be told what an AD was, or why a broken lunch was a matter of such importance. (An AD is an Assistant Director, who usually deals with the extras, and a broken lunch—a postponed lunch-break—means a little more money.) It was also very soothing about my brush with Wardrobe, agreeing that 'funky' was possibly the least helpful description that it had ever heard.

'Would you like to hear a story tonight?'

17

it enquired when I was sufficiently soothed. 'I have a very nice romantic one about a mummy.'

The chimaera obviously wanted to tell it, so I said that I would like to hear it, as I was already growing fond of the little creature, and I did not want to hurt its feelings. But I was by no means confident that a story about a mummy would be either nice or romantic.

Although as it turned out I was quite wrong.

IN THE MUSEUM

'Mr Westbury,' said Laura, wearily, 'has been *dancing* at the mummies again.'

Laura liked her job in the museum. It was only sometimes that things got too much for her, but today had definitely been one of those times. She had not even been able to slip out for a quiet sit down and a coffee in her favourite little cafe at lunchtime. Lily Waters, who was one of those eccentrics (like Mr Westbury!) who seemed drawn to the Museum like wasps to a picnic, and where they were just about as welcome, had seen her crossing the forecourt, and hailed her in that foghorn voice of hers.

Laura could hardly pretend that she had not seen her. Lily's figure was as unmistakeable as her voice. She wore three layers of coats, winter and summer, none of which had actually been intended to fit her frankly cuboid shape, and a woollen hat that looked very like a tea-cosy. Indeed, if Lily wore it at a certain angle you could see that it really was—or had been—a tea cosy. The hole for the handle had been inexpertly sewn up but the smaller spout hole was left open, perhaps for ventilation.

But Lily was no ordinary bag lady. At first Laura had thought that she came into the Museum every day because it offered somewhere warm and relatively quiet to sit, but one day Lily had explained that she really came to visit friends. She had, apparently, been a priestess in Atlantis, and from there she had worked her way through a variety of exciting incarnations, during which she had come to know many of the exhibits in the Museum personally. She was able to tell Laura a great many details of their private lives, few of which appeared on the white cards describing their careers for the ordinary Museum visitor.

Privately Laura felt that Lily's versions were often more interesting than the official one. 'She was a Sarky Cow,' she would announce in her grating tones as she stood in front of the sarcophagus of the High Priestess of Bast, Ra Hoshet, 'but her auntie, Ka Hoshet, now she was a real sweetie.' All in all Lily was a strong personality and it was not surprising that Laura found herself swept helplessly along beside her into a nasty little pub instead of a

19

nice little cafe.

She also found herself telling Lily about her problems with Mr Westbury.

Lily clicked her tongue. She had little patience with eccentricity, unless it was her own, and she was extremely possessive about the mummies.

'What's he want to dance at them for?' she demanded.

'He thinks,' said Laura, still more wearily, 'that if he performs a certain ritual dance in front of the right mummy he will revive his one true love, the Princess Ne Nu Fa. The only problem, well, the only problem as far as he's concerned, is that he's not quite sure which one she is. He thinks we've got our labelling wrong.'

Lily gave a little huff of agreement.

Laura chose to ignore this and went on, 'So he keeps trying out his dance in front of different mummies. And today a school party came in while he was at it and they joined in.'

'What, they all started dancing?'

'Yes. Some of them were very good,' she admitted, reluctantly, 'quite professional. Break-dancing they call it, I think, and well they might. It was sheer luck that nothing *did* get broken. I really don't know what the Co-Ordinator would have said if he'd seen it.'

'I expect he kept well out of the way, until you'd dealt with things,' said Lily shrewdly. 'You know, dearie, there's such a thing as being too efficient. You want to tell him you can't cope sometimes. Burst into tears. He might just sweep you into his arms.'

'I don't want him to sweep me into his arms,' Laura said, lying through her teeth. 'I just want to get on with my job.'

Lily sniffed incredulously. And she was right to do so. Laura was in love with the Co-Ordinator. But she was quite, quite certain that if she ever did burst into tears in his presence he would not sweep her into his arms and beg her not to cry. He was far more likely to throw a glass of water over her and call the keepers to take her away. She swallowed the last of her bitter lemon and put the glass down firmly, indicating that she was ready to get up. But Lily paid never paid attention to non-verbal cues. And she knew to the minute what time Laura had to be back at her desk.

'You've got a really powerful aura today, you know, love,' she stated. 'Fairly shooting out golden rays you are.'

Several customers glanced round nervously and the barman leaned forward hopefully. He had never had to ask someone to leave because her aura was disturbing the other customers, but there was always a first time.

'It's spreading round you like great golden wings,' said Lily, becoming lyrical under the influence of a small port and lemon. 'This is really going to be your lucky day.'

Laura, muttering that if this were true she

21

hoped she never had an unlucky one, managed to get up and gather up her coat and bag. Lily stood up too. There seemed no way of shaking her off without being unacceptably rude, and Laura was incapable of rudeness. She might be an eccentric old spinster herself, any day now, she reminded herself.

'Let's have a walk through the Mummy Gallery,' said Lily, 'you've got ten minutes before you have to be back in your office.'

The Gallery was almost empty. Almost but not quite. A small, shabby figure, with drooping shoulders stood in front of one of the mummy cases. Laura, with a sinking heart, recognised Mr Westbury. She braced herself to get him out quickly and quietly before he could start his ritual dance again, but she had hardly moved a step when Lily gave a great cry in a voice that no longer sounded like a fog-horn, but like a great golden bell.

And Mr Westbury, looking round at her, echoed that cry, bronze to Lily's gold. Laura had not understood what Lily said, she only caught the meaning of joy and recognition. But she heard Mr Westbury quite clearly.

He had called 'Ne Nu Fa!'

The two silly, shabby figures moved towards each other, their silliness and shabbiness falling away as they moved. A tall, bronze man, beautiful as any statue in the Ancient Greek collection (and quite as naked, a dazed Laura noticed), met and embraced a golden woman in a dazzle of light. There was music too, and a wave of perfume, like a spring morning. And then, suddenly, there was nothing. The Gallery was empty in the grey light of an autumn afternoon, empty except for Laura, shaking and weeping, and the Co-Ordinator, who had rushed out of his office, thinking, as he afterwards explained, that the Museum was on fire. He gathered the sobbing Laura into his arms without hesitation, murmuring: 'There, there Miss Wilson. Please don't cry.'

And Laura raised her swimming eyes to his face and said: 'Please—call me Laura.'

'Laura,' said the Co-Ordinator wonderingly, and, quite unaware that the Mummy Gallery had begun to fill up, he kissed her in front of a fascinated audience, which by then included twenty-five mixed infants, four teachers and the Keeper of the Gallery.

Much later, when they were talking, as newly married couples will, of the events that had brought them together, the Co-Ordinator was inclined to deny that anything supernatural had happened at all. The music they had heard had come from Mr Westbury's mini tape-recorder, which he had smuggled in, as usual, under his coat. The light must have been caused by one of those mysterious surges of electricity which had caused havoc with the computers on several occasions. And the fact that neither Lily nor Mr Westbury had ever been seen again in the Museum (nor anywhere else—for Laura had made discreet enquiries), well, that was pure coincidence.

'Anyway, the whole thing just doesn't make sense, not even in supernatural terms. Lily wasn't a mummy, was she, so Mr Westbury couldn't have revived her. Besides, Ne Nu Fa isn't an Egyptian name at all. It sounds just like nenuphar to me, and that means waterlily.'

'Waterlily. Lily Waters,' said Laura thoughtfully.

But she said it to herself.

'Now, this will interest you,' said her husband, cosily changing the subject, as even newly married husbands will, to more practical affairs. 'Someone who's been with an American expedition in Egypt has found a scroll which gives some background on one of our exhibits. You know, Ra Hoshet, High Priestess of Bast.'

'What does it say about her?' Laura asked.

'Well, it seems she wasn't much liked. She took over from her aunt, who had been a very popular lady, apparently, and it seems to have caused a bit of a flutter in the temple dovecot, if you see what I mean.'

He began to translate from the hieroglyphics which had been reproduced in the magazine he was reading. 'Ra Hoshet, the sharp-speaking . . . er . . . this is rather a rude term I think . . . it could mean something like "holy female monster" . . . she was the daughter of the sister of the . . . er . . . honey-mouthed Ka Hoshet who was also a High Priestess of Bast.'

Laura sat up abruptly. 'Could that mean 'She was a Sarky Cow, but her auntie, Ka Hoshet, was a real sweetie?' she said.

He beamed. 'Do you know, I think that's exactly what it does mean. Rather a clever colloquial translation, darling.'

'It was Lily's translation, not mine.'

'But that's not possible. As I said, the papyrus has only just come to light. Literally. There is no way that Lily could have seen it.'

They stared at each other.

'Lily *did* know Ra Hoshet. And her auntie. And she and Mr Westbury *were* lovers. Perhaps it *was* in Atlantis. Somewhere in all the lifetimes they lost track of each other. And Mr Westbury forgot the details. As you would. But he knew he'd lost someone. And he recognised her when he found her again.'

Her husband smiled fondly at this uncharacteristic whimsy and took her hands. 'I hope we never lose each other,' he said seriously.

'Oh, no, we'll never do that,' Laura said confidently. She could feel her aura embracing them both, like great golden wings.

'And did they live happily ever after?' I asked the chimaera.

'Of course,' it said confidently. 'People in stories always do.'

'Not in my stories,' I said.

25

The chimaera was too polite to reply, but its expression suggested that there might be a reason here for my signal lack of success in getting anything published.

THE THIRD STORY

I had a most unexpected piece of luck one day in that long summer when I had a chimaera living in my wardrobe. I actually got one of the photographic jobs my agency sent me for, so, for a morning spent being photographed wearing a peculiarly unbecoming overall, clutching a mop (and jumping wildly into the air) I would earn quite a reasonable sum, and have a free afternoon. Of course, I had many free afternoons, but they were usually accompanied by free mornings and no money at all, so this one felt like a holiday. I bought a bag of cherries, which were just coming into season, on my way home, and arrived moments before the weather broke in a kind of tropical storm.

I sat with the chimaera, watching the solid sheets of rain shatter themselves against the pavement far below and eating cherries. Well, the chimaera did not actually eat them, but it played with some, rather cutely, tossing them about with its little goat hooves. When the fruit was finished I found my sketchpad and tried to draw a simplified outline of the chimaera, with the idea that I might transfer it to a cushion cover, and embroider it. I was a little worried that it might be fading, but it seemed satisfactorily solid, and, when it saw what I was doing, it adopted a series of helpful poses until we found the right one. Then, while I sketched, it told me a story.

Evening was our usual story time but it had been infected by the holiday atmosphere. This was the story it told on that rainy afternoon. Perhaps it had also been affected by the sight of all that water because the title of the story was:

FROG

'This is going to be a very difficult letter. You see, I don't really know where to start, or even who to address. Dear everyone, I suppose. Well then—Dear everyone—I'm really sorry. No, truly I am. I know you did your best for me, and don't think that I'm not grateful. You stood by me when the tabloids mounted that campaign suggesting that I'd left eight hundred fatherless tadpoles in the Well at the World's End, and you said that DNA tests wouldn't be necessary to disprove the allegations, although I was perfectly willing to take them.'

The prince sat back for a moment, staring

down at the thick, marbled paper. And was that because they really did trust me, he wondered, or because they were afraid the tests might show that those tadpoles were my offspring? After all I was in that well for a hundred years, and a frog can get pretty lonely—am I sure even now that those tests would have put me in the clear? He sighed, and started to write again.

'And when that cable channel wheeled out Sir Mortimer Groaning, the pop-genealogist, who said that in spite of my having clearly undergone a successful transformation there was always a chance that I would introduce frog-genes into the royal blood-line, you came right out there, fighting for me . . .'

Although perhaps it might have been done with more, well, sensitivity. He remembered his then future father-in-law shouting at his fainting then future mother-in-law, who'd had a preview of the tapes.

'For Heaven's sake woman! Look at your own family, I mean look at them with an unprejudiced eye, and tell me that most of them wouldn't be improved by the addition of a few frog-genes. I mean to say, frog-genes aren't the worst thing in your blood-line, if you'll allow me to remind you of it. Look at your aunt Ethelburga. I know your family always told everyone that she was rescued by young Siegfried from that dragon just in the nick of time, but I'm not so sure of that.

28

Oh, I know, they arranged a quick wedding, because of course it was love at first sight, *they said*, and then a good long honeymoon to allow them both to recover from their ordeal, and lo and behold they come back from a year in the wilds of Ruritania with those triplets. Well, they could be Siegfried's I suppose, he was no oil painting, but I do have to say that Franz and Ernst are the only young men of my acquaintance who have never needed to borrow a cigar lighter. And that girl, Ethelinda, she's got scales! Iridescent green scales!—Not unattractive, in an odd sort of way,' he added thoughtfully.

His then future mother-in-law muttered something into her sodden handkerchief.

'Yes, madam, I do know that your mutual great-grandmother was a mermaid, but it seems very odd to me that scales haven't come out in any other part of the family. And you are not going to tell me, I hope, that she was also a *fire-breathing* mermaid!'

The prince smiled wryly. His now never-to-be father-in-law had not really liked him any more than the rest of the family had. But he loved his daughter and the circumstances of his transformation had been, well, even in this day and age, just a tad unfortunate. The old man might even have been grateful that he was so anxious to go through with the wedding. There can be few fathers who react with delight when they discover that their only daughter's pet frog has turned into a young man overnight, especially when she has chosen to keep him in her bedroom . . . on her pillow. Not that the princess had seemed to mind at the time . . . but he mustn't think about her. He went back to his letter:

'In fact, you all did your best to make me welcome and I know that it's my fault that I just didn't fit in. I did my best too, but I'm afraid that a hundred years in the Well at the World's End hasn't really fitted me for a life in the spot-light. There always seems to be so much to do here—'

Always, he thought, an abattoir to open, or some provincial mayor to engage in stilted conversation, or some deadly dull state function to attend. But he might have been able to put up with it all, even the mayors and the abattoirs if—but when he'd seen her stricken face tonight—it was tonight's banquet which had finally finished him, of course.

'—and I've come to believe that I'm just not the right person to do it. It wasn't really the incident tonight. That was no one's fault, and I'm sure—'

Well, it was someone's fault actually. He'd seen Franz and Ernst, sniggering in those long moustaches they wore to conceal their ever-so-slightly non-human dentition, just before the man-servant had lifted the lid on the dish he was presenting to him to reveal—frog's legs! He couldn't help it. He'd rushed from

30

the table, and later sent a message that he was too ill to join the rest of the family at the grand ball. And then he'd locked his bedroom door, and, in fear and hope, he'd sat on his bed and dialed a certain number. Would she be at home? Would she, after all this time, still be alive? And if at home and alive, would she be willing to help?

He tried to remember the exact circumstances of his transfrogmification. Everyone—even the tabloids and the satellite channels had assumed that it was a christening curse: some bad-tempered old bat whose invitation had gone astray in the post had turned up at the ceremony anyway and given the baby webbed feet. It happened every day. Well, not quite *every* day. Well, every hundred years, and mostly in royal circles but it did happen. The trouble was, he didn't think it had been quite like that. A hundred years is a long time, but he had a feeling that it had been more—personal. And that he hadn't been a baby—and she hadn't been an old hag at all . . . the phone was still ringing. She wasn't going to be there . . . and then someone picked up the receiver at the other end of the line.

'Had enough, have you then?' she had asked in that achingly familiar voice, even before he told her who was speaking. 'Thought you might. Well, I can transform you into a frog again, but that'll be it. A frog you'll be and a frog you'll stay. No more disenchantment for

31

you my lad.'

'That's just what I want,' he said.

'Quite sure?'

'Quite sure,' he echoed desolately.

'All right then. Here's what you do—'

He looked at his letter. It already said too much, and at the same time not nearly enough. Abruptly he picked up his pen and scrawled:

'Sorry again. Love you all. Don't try to find me. Good bye.'

Then he went out onto his balcony. It was an easy jump to the garden, particularly for him. He was very good at jumping. Following the witch's instructions, he walked quietly over the dew-wet lawn. The Well moved about a bit, and just now, he had been promised it would be at the end of the palace gardens. He thought, as he had found himself doing so often recently, of his years in the Well. It was astonishing how much time you could spend watching cloud shadows on water. And leaves. It was true, that old saying that no two leaves are alike. And of course there were more exciting times: fierce crystal days of frost when the edges of the Well crisped into ice, and, almost best of all, those long still evenings at the end of a hot day, when the upper part of the Well water was almost the same temperature as the cooling air, and you could lie on a lily leaf, not sure if you were in water or sky . . . For a moment he hesitated, gazing back at the darkened palace—thinking how much he had wished he could show his princess just how wonderful his Well had been—and then a rustle in the bushes jerked him back to the present.

He rather hoped it was Franz or Ernst. No one was going to stop him now, and he would much prefer to clobber either, or both of those gentlemen than an innocent palace guard. But then a bright head emerged from the undergrowth, followed by a pair of pale shoulders and a white satin dress.

'Where are you going?' hissed his betrothed.

'I'm going back to the Well,' he said desperately. 'I must. It would never have worked.'

'It won't work here,' she agreed. 'That's why I'm coming with you.'

'What!'

'You want to be a frog, I'll be a frog. That's what marriage is about, after all.'

'But the kingdom—'

'Let Franz and Ernst fight over it if they want it. If anyone will let them, after the scandal.'

'What scandal?' he asked.

'The scandal which is going to break in tomorrow's papers. I phoned them after the—incident—and some other—people too. You see, Aunt Ethelburga's dragon had a mate. She was brooding her eggs at the time, which perhaps accounted for the thing with Aunt Ethelburga, and in spite of the trauma she managed to hatch them all. Two boys and a girl. Apparently this is what dragons usually produce. The boys don't want to talk, they're willing to let bygones be etc, typical male, but the girl will. She is, she claims, Franz and Ernst's half-sister. And she'll take a blood-test to prove it. *And* she'll do topless pix if the price is right.'

'Topless?' he said blankly.

'Dragons,' she said, 'are rather unusual. They hatch their young out of eggs, but they also suckle them. And this young female is quite—sinuous. I understand that she has six outstanding reasons for being an extremely desirable addition to page three of one of our most popular tabloids.'

'Six?'

'Six. Dragons have six.'

'Does Ethelinda—?'

'No one knows—but she's never appeared in public wearing a bikini—of course, that could be because of the scales.'

'How did you find out about—all this?'

'We've always known, but until tonight I was ready to go along with the family cover-up. Until I saw your face when he took the cover off that dish. Then I made those calls.'

'But—I thought when I looked at you that you'd given up on me.'

'No. I'd given up on *them*.'

He whistled softly. 'Are you sure you want to be a frog? I mean, the Well at the World's

End can be very quiet—'

'Yes,' she said firmly. 'I've burned my boats really. I want to spend a hundred years with you, watching cloud shadows.'

'I never thought you were listening when I told you about them.'

'I was listening all right. What do we have to do?'

'The witch said: Follow the Silver Road across the lawn.'

'Silver road?'

'Snail trails,' he said prosaically. 'They'll lead us to the Well, and by the time we get there—'

'We'll have changed.'

She hauled up her satin skirts and led the way, peering at the grass for snail tracks. He followed her, completely taken aback by this turn of events. As they walked towards the Well the sky began to lighten. The tiny trails of snail slime glowed, glittered and expanded. They really were following a Silver Road. And as the witch had promised, the Change began to happen. His horrible dry skin became cool and delicious, another whole organ of sensation: he could feel the freshening morning air, and the sweetness of the dewy grass in every exquisite inch of it; his clumsy feet and hands became delicate webbed paws—he hopped free of his banqueting clothes and glanced nervously towards his betrothed. Her dress lay on the grass, and the

35

most beautiful lady frog he had ever seen was negligently disengaging herself from a pearl necklace.

'Do I look all right?' she asked shyly.

'You look—wonderful.'

He kissed her emerald snout, and paw in webby paw they scurried towards the Well, reaching the curb just as the sun rose. They dived into its wonderful, cool mysterious depths—and vanished for ever from mortal sight.

To live, happy for ever ever after.

*   *   *

The chimaera gave a little sigh of pleasure. It clearly liked happy endings.

'So that's what really happened to the Frog Prince,' I said. 'But—why *was* he turned into a frog? And who did it?'

'A witch—well a very powerful enchantress really—did it. But I couldn't tell you why. It was, as he said, very personal.'

I nodded. Some secrets are best kept untold.

'But—was it definitely an enchantress and not a fairy? It's odd, but fairies so rarely do turn up in fairy stories.'

The chimaera's cherry-amber eyes shone with amusement. 'That's because they're not stories *about* fairies,' it said. 'They're stories *by* fairies *about* humans.'

And if you think about it, that does make a

good deal of sense.

THE FOURTH STORY

The rain-storm did not mark the end of the hot weather. It grew hotter than ever over the next week and I was almost relieved that I did not have to spend whole days on a film set. I did, however go to several castings. I had little expectation of getting the jobs I went for, and in fact I did not, but I met several people I knew and we all went for coffee afterwards and caught up on all the gossip.

I told the chimaera some of the stories I had heard, and he volunteered to tell me a much stranger one than those I had been exchanging with my colleagues. I said I would be very pleased to hear it, and while I worked on my chimaera embroidery he told me the story of:

STAGE STRUCK

Martin climbed the one hundred and seventeen steps—concrete, painted a dark institutional green—which led up to the casting studio. When he opened the door his heart, never particularly buoyant about castings, sank right down to his trainers. The tiny waiting room was already full of people. The Agencies were obviously parading the usual suspects: Mark, Harry, Jake, Phil, someone, who was vaguely familiar, and someone else he was sure he'd worked with on something, and whatshisname were already sitting round the walls, perched on folding chairs. They were telling each other lies about previous jobs, between anxiously asking each other if anyone 'knew what they were looking for.'

Martin suppressed a nasty impulse to announce that he had been told to prepare a tap-dance routine (he hadn't, but it might cause a bit of alarm and despondency). He looked round for a free chair. There wasn't one.

'They must be taking an awfully long time with each person,' he said, unhappily. 'What are they doing in there?'

'They're not here yet,' said Harry. 'They haven't even started. Damn nuisance. I've got another casting at half-past-three.'

Harry always had another casting that he had to get to. Sometimes, on his bad days, Martin thought that might be true.

'Saw your ad,' whatshisname volunteered. 'Who got you that?'

Martin ran a swift mental show-reel of work he had done in the last eighteen months and decided he didn't have the faintest idea what the man was talking about. Unless being momentarily and embarrassingly visible in a crowd waving what appeared to be giant orange phalluses, advertising something he couldn't remember counted as 'his ad.' He smiled vaguely and tried to find somewhere to put his bag. They—or rather he—the others might have been told something quite different—had been asked to bring a change of tops. One of his possible changes was a pyjama jacket, but he thought it might pass for a shirt. At least, unlike his selection of real shirts, it was clean and not actually falling to pieces.

The conversation had veered to 'old so-and-so' who had been paid an astronomical sum—plus repeat fees—for his appearance in an advertisement for lavatory cleanser. He would go through the rest of his life under the name of Dan-Dan the Lavatory Man, but still . . .

'Just pulled him out of the crowd,' said Phil, in hushed tones. 'There was a problem with the one they'd cast—didn't turn up, or something and the director said "He'll do" and they got him to phone the Agency on his mobile and negotiate the fee there and then.' He shook his head. 'Went out thinking he was going to do a day's background and went home dunno how many thousand pounds better off.'

'Of course,' Mark said, trying to keep a note of satisfaction out of his voice, 'he'll never work again. He'll always be Dan-Dan . . .'

'No. He's got a pantomime,' said someone authoritatively. 'In the North.'

'Doing what?' Martin asked.

'Some version of Aladdin. He's playing the character formerly known as Wishee Washee.'

'Oh, don't tell me,' said Harry. 'Now called Dan-Dan . . .'

'The Lavatory Man,' the room chorused.

A small, eager face surrounded by bunches of electric hair suddenly appeared at the glass partition which separated the waiting room from the office and everyone fell silent.

'Gentlemen, I'm ever so sorree,' the face announced, 'but we're running late. I've just had a phone-call. We're going to have to put everything back a bit. If you'd like to go off and have a coffee and come back in twenty minutes . . .' the rest of her words, if any, were lost in the crash of folding chairs as the room emptied. Well, not quite emptied. As Martin left the room he heard Harry protesting querulously that he must insist on being seen first as soon as they arrived, he had another appointment . . .

Martin wandered down the stairs, choosing not to join the general rush. He wondered if it was really worth coming back. Almost certainly it wasn't, but again, almost certainly he would. As he turned onto the second landing he almost ran into the someone he vaguely remembered working with. He was leaning against the wall and panting gently.

'Are you all right?' Martin asked.

'Fine, fine,' he wheezed. 'Just getting a bit

40

old for this kind of thing.'

'There's a coffee-shop on the corner,' Martin said. 'Just down the street. We might as well go there and you can sit down.' He wondered if he ought to offer the man his arm, but it might look a bit odd. Besides he seemed to have perked up a bit. He followed Martin quite nimbly down the rest of the stairs and down the street to the coffee shop. Ahead a phalanx of their fellow actors could be seen making for a pub called *The Green Man and Curling Tongs*, which seemed to Martin to be a very bad idea, less for the effect it might have on any subsequent performance at the audition than from the risk of having to spend money.

They established themselves at an outside table and the other, who seemed to have recovered completely, nipped inside.

'I ordered cappuccino,' he announced on emerging. 'Hope that's OK.'

'Thanks,' said Martin.

There was a rather awkward silence, and then Martin exclaimed 'Exeter! I'm sure I worked with you in Exeter!'

The man looked rather taken aback. 'I *have* worked in Exeter. Did my first job there, but I'm not sure . . .'

'No . . . perhaps not . . . sorry. But I'm sure I have worked with you . . .' And then he jumped. He felt something brush his ankle, as if a dog or a cat had sidled up to him, but when

41

he glanced down there was nothing there. There was no chance that his companion was playing footsie either (not that Martin thought there was much chance of that anyway, but in this profession you never knew). Both his feet, rather small for a man, and curiously trotterish in their brightly polished shoes were set decorously on the pavement at such an angle that he'd have to be a contortionist to try anything like that. Besides he was talking quite calmly.

'Oh, you probably have worked with me,' he was saying, 'pretty well everyone has.'

A girl came out with two thick mugs full of brown foam and set them on the table. She did not wait for any money so perhaps the other had already paid. Martin wondered if he should offer him some cash, or offer to buy another round—well—better play it by ear. He picked up his cup and took a sip of coffee. It was, unusually for cappuccino, scalding hot, and he put it down hastily.

'Do you hail from the West Country?' he said.

'No. No, more the North if anywhere,' the man said. 'Why? Do I have a western burr?' he added, sounding a little put out.

'No, just that you said you started work in Exeter.'

'Ah. Ah. Yes. Indeed I did. In *The Tragedy of Dr Faustus*.'

'Theatre in Education was it?' Martin said

sympathetically.

'Ah no. It was a tour. It began in London, but I—er—joined the cast in Exeter.'

Something cold touched the back of Martin's neck. He was a bit of a theatre historian, and there was something, something about Exeter and Faust, something . . . Ah. In 1593 the Lord Admiral's Men had been touring with Faust, and in Exeter they discovered they had one devil more than they bargained for in the cast. A real devil. He looked up. 'When was this?'

'Oh, a long time ago. It was only a one-night performance, but—I was bitten by the theatre bug. I've been in theatre ever since.'

'Four hundred years ago?' said Martin, not really believing it, but oddly enough at the same time he was not really surprised when his companion said, 'Give or take. I—er—left the cast in Exeter. Well, in Exeter Cathedral to be precise, on their knees. I went to London.'

'Did you ever meet . . .?' Martin asked breathlessly.

'Will? Everyone asks that of course. Well, yes I did. Gave him a few hints, you know. He paid me a rather nice compliment in one of his plays.'

'The Prince of Darkness is a gentleman?' Martin hazarded.

The man—er—demon—nodded rather complacently.

Then he looked a little uneasy. 'Of course

that made me feel worse about—well—the incident. *Henry VIII.*'

'You mean when the theatre burned down?' said Martin.

He nodded. 'I'm afraid that's the kind of thing that tends to happen when I'm in a production.'

'Oh dear,' said Martin inadequately.

'Still. I haven't let it get me down. I don't think I've been out of work for—well—more than a few months at a time since Exeter. Of course there was a bit of hiatus in Oliver's time, but there were private performances even then. Oliver himself liked opera, or what passed for opera then . . . and then the theatres opened again. They always do, somehow. And I've . . . adapted.'

Fascinated, Martin watched a series—not of expressions but of actual faces pass in front of him: a pale, rather fine featured face with a small pointed black beard, dissolved into a looser coarser version then changed into a rouged and doll-like mask (eighteenth century he supposed), a beardless, altogether more rugged look for the nineteenth century and then the modern face he almost recognised.

He picked up his coffee cup for a reviving sip, but the liquid was still quite literally boiling. The demon, seeing him wince, pointed a long finger at it, and it transformed into a glass of iced coffee.

'Oh, sorry—overdone it as usual,' he

muttered.

'No, no really this is fine,' Martin said hastily.

'Now, of course,' the demon continued, 'there's film and television, but—the basics don't change.'

Martin felt that nudge at his ankle again and glanced down, to see, without surprise, a muscular tail fitted with a neat sharp barb, whisking about under the table. 'I suppose you've worked with all the greats . . .' he said.

'Well. Not as such. Somehow I always seem to do second tours. I mean—I *saw* them of course. Garrick. Irving.'

'Did you give Irving any hints? He actually played Mephistopheles, didn't he . . .'

'Irving,' said the demon, with a hint of admiration, 'was impervious to hints. But I think I was quite helpful to his business manager.'

'You mean Stoker . . .' Martin began excitedly.

The demon winked and lifted a lip briefly to expose a very sharp canine tooth. 'I like to think that Mr Stoker's Dracula owed something to my goodself.' Then he sighed. 'I've done the odd bit of backstage of course. The nineteenth century! Ah that was the time for special effects. Pyrotechnics,' he sighed again. 'And I suppose I could have made it big then on stage. Lot of parts for demons. But . . . I always wanted a challenge. We all

45

like to be cast against type I suppose and I always fancied playing the good guy. And it's all realism now, of course. Still. I get on. I do quite a bit of background. I can blend in well, you see. Ah well. Live in hopes, eh?'

He gathered up his tail and slipped the barb into his jacket pocket, where it seemed, somehow to blend in with his clothes and vanish.

'So. You've never actually—well—made it?'

'Not yet,' said the devil seriously. 'Not yet. Well, we'd better be getting back.' He swigged off his coffee and stood up.

Martin, after only a moment's hesitation did the same.

*   *   *

'I'm not absolutely sure I like that story,' I said, thinking about it. 'Four hundred years in the business, and never making it . . . Did Martin get the casting?'

'No. No one did. The client changed his mind, and they called a different set of people in. But Martin got quite friendly with the demon and had long conversations with him on various shoots. Eventually he wrote a very successful series of historical novels about an Italian actor, Niccolo Vecchio who comes to England in Elizabethan times with a troupe of actors, changes his name to Nick Vickers, and founds a theatrical dynasty, all based on stories

46

the demon had told him.'

I stared at the chimaera. I knew the Niccolo Vecchio books well. They were very long, very elaborate, and very interesting, huge doorsteps of books, with lushly coloured covers. If anyone was reading a book on a shoot, ten to one it would be a Niccolo Vecchio novel.

Critics admired their historical detail. Actors admired their realism. 'It must have been just like that!' they would exclaim . . . I could not, off-hand, remember the name of the author, but I was sure it was not Martin. Not that that meant anything. I was certainly not going to write under the name I used for my agency work. The chimaera looked back at me, with an innocent expression.

'Can I see how your embroidery is going?' it asked.

I showed it. 'You haven't made me look very fierce,' it said, sounding a little disappointed.

I didn't like to say that it didn't look very fierce. Cute, or cuddly, but definitely not fierce . . . but the chimaera, like the rest of us, obviously yearned to work against type. 'I wasn't trying for fierce,' I told it. 'I wanted to catch your—er—classic dignity. Fierce is not good for cushion covers.'

The chimaera repeated 'Classic dignity,' and preened. It seemed happy with that.

'Did the Niccolo Vecchio author really get his historical details from a stage-struck devil?' I asked.

47

The chimaera grinned. 'Well—Niccolo Vecchio does mean Old Nick,' he pointed out. 'In Italian.'

And so it does.

THE FIFTH STORY

One day I came home in a very depressed mood. I had been depressed enough before I went out, because one of my short stories had come back to me, not with a standard rejection slip, saying politely that it was not quite right for the magazine I had sent it to (which was the kind of thing I was quite used to) but with a very detailed piece of criticism from the editor. I think she had meant to be helpful, but she mentioned (among other things) that my characters, who were faithful representations of people I had met on various shoots, were 'too fantastic, and quite lacking in any kind of reality.'

Then I had gone out to register with a new agency, and they had been sniffy about my eight by tens. (That is, my professionally taken head-shots, which I had been rather pleased with . . .) Indeed, the girl who looked at my photographs had used the dreadfully damning phrase 'a strong look'. Now, this does not actually mean 'hideously ugly' as I had thought at first. I have heard it used about a quite beautiful model. But it does mean 'hard to place.' They did agree to put me on their books, but I left feeling bruised and unhappy. I had no immediate prospect of work, and I was becoming worried about the rent. I did not want to find myself turned out onto the streets, especially now I had a chimaera to look after—I had unhappy fantasies of having to leave it in a box on the door-step of the local Cat Rescuers, a solution which I feared would satisfy no one, least of all probably, the Cat Rescuers.

But the chimaera was very supportive. It said if I did have to leave my attic it would be quite happy to wear a collar and lead, and hide its snaky hindquarters during the day, under a coat or a blanket, so it could pass for a rather exotic dog, while I busked, or sold copies of *The Big Issue*. And at night, while I was sleeping in a cardboard box it could stand guard. It was small, it agreed, but as a fabulous beast it could melt into cloud, when kicked, and a boot would go harmlessly through it, but once it had re-formed it could guarantee that its teeth could go right through that boot, indeed, it sounded as if it were quite looking forward to the prospect. I was already beginning to feel better, as I felt we were making sensible contingency plans—and besides I knew, when I thought about it soberly, that I had money to come in, and the rent was probably safe for a month or so anyway. And as for the 'strong look', the chimaera, who had something of a strong look itself, protested that this was nothing to worry about at all.

'I could tell you a story about someone who really did have a strong look,' it offered.

So I made us some tea, got out my embroidery, and settled down to listen to:

A STRONG LOOK

Sergeant Prendergast and his partner PC Oliver were drinking cups of some kind of hot bitter brown liquid (possibly tea) at a coffee-stall much patronised by bikers. The Sergeant had also risked a hot meat pie, and was currently immersed in gravy up to the ears, and unable to return the jovial greetings of the biking fraternity, except by enthusiastic hand movements. PC Oliver was horrified to see how many of the bikers seemed to know his superior officer very well, addressing him familiarly as 'Bazza', but he knew if he expressed his horror the Sergeant would protest that he was practising 'community policing.'

Most of the bikers seemed to be big hirsute men of the kind who look as if they do not know quite what to do with their hands if they do not have a battle-axe to swing, and some of them carried equally formidable ladies on their pillions. Although a few of the ladies were really quite toothsome . . . PC Oliver found himself gazing at a svelte figure in black leathers perched behind someone roughly the size and shape of a barn door who looked as if he ought to be called 'Thorfinn'. Her face was completely hidden under her helmet, of course, but her figure was definitely . . . there was something about black leather, especially when it clung like that . . .

A gravy-stained fist hit him squarely between the shoulder blades. 'Don't even think about it, boy,' Sergeant Prendergast, who had disposed of his pie, roared jovially. 'She's right out of your league.'

PC Oliver tried to think of something to say that would not make him sound like a spinster aunt, then gave it up. 'Shouldn't we be getting back to the car, sir?' he asked.

'Now that's the trouble with you young coppers,' the Sergeant boomed. 'You stick in your vehicles like—like . . .' (he searched for a suitable simile, and gave up) 'like—limpets. You never want to come out and get to know the public. It's them that pay your wages, lad, and don't you forget it.'

PC Oliver forbore to point out that in the event of a vote for 'Man Least Likely to Leave his Patrol Car (Even if it Was on Fire)' Sergeant Prendergast would undoubtedly sweep the poll. Instead he let his eyes wander

51

back to the lithe lady in leather. With some idea of distracting his sergeant from this, he said, 'Are there always this many bikers here?'

'No, lad. They've come for the art exhibition.'

'Art exhibition?' PC Oliver repeated.

'Art exhibition,' Sergeant Prendergast said again, rolling the words round his mouth. 'You see. That proves my point. If you did more community coppering you'd know what was going on in your patch.'

'Well, what is going on then?' Oliver snapped.

Sergeant Prendergast spun his empty cup round by the handle and exclaimed, whimsically, 'Oh, dear. My cup appears to be empty. Your turn to get them in, I think.'

It always was his turn of course. PC Oliver took both empty cups and plodded towards the coffee stall. The crowd parted good naturedly enough to let him through, which was perhaps lucky because he wasn't really looking where he was going—he was gazing back at the young lady who had first caught his attention. Perhaps she was an artist's model, he thought—if the old walrus was telling the truth about them all being there for an art exhibition, of course. It might be worth going along if there was a portrait of her—without her leathers, as it were. He pulled his thoughts back from that dangerous avenue, bought two more cups of thick dark tea, added the statutory two large spoonfuls of sugar to one of them, and made his way back to Sergeant Prendergast. That gentleman was now in close and apparently confidential conversation with the large bearded man who had been carrying the current object of PC Oliver's fancy on his pillion. On closer inspection he looked even bigger than PC Oliver had thought, and he appeared to be dressed, at least as far as his upper body went, mainly in tattoos. Oliver hung back but the Sergeant waved him on.

'Jack here'll tell you about the exhibition,' he roared, accepting his cup with some suspicion. 'I hope you've given this a proper stir, lad, you know I hate getting a mouthful of sugar right at the end.'

Oliver turned to Jack and eyed him narrowly. Recent events had made him rather suspicious of his Sergeant. He seemed to know some very odd people indeed. He wondered if 'Jack' could be a werewolf (he was certainly hairy enough), an avatar of Thor, or perhaps a reincarnation of one of the more famous figures from local history, Olaf the Strange, a Viking who, on recovering from a massive head-injury inflicted with an axe at the Battle of Blackwater had become an early environmentalist, and vegetarian . . . but in fact, apart from the tattoos he seemed human enough. True it was not an especially warm day, and he was wearing a leather waistcoat that left his arms, chest and shoulders bare, allowing the green and blue snakes that rioted down his arms to appear in their full glory . . . he was, obviously, a snake man. The back of his waistcoat was decorated with a huge painting of a woman's face—but a woman with snakes instead of hair.

'I suppose you're an artist then?' PC Oliver said, with fine irony.

Jack rumbled with what appeared to be good-natured laughter, but Sergeant Prendergast said, 'No, lad. He's an exhibit.'

PC Oliver felt his jaw drop, but Sergeant Prendergast abruptly took pity on his junior. 'It's very modern lad. Something they call conceptual art. They're holding it at the Town Hall.'

'Ah.' Everything was explained. Anything might happen at the Town Hall, where the Council was Modern and Progressive. An Art Exhibition consisting of real bikers (would they be expected to stand quite still, like living statues, he wondered? or would they just wander about, so you would only realise they were works of art if you were in the know?) was nothing to some of things the Council had sponsored. He was suddenly conscious that the low rumbling sound, which had started up in the region of his left ear, was not a motorbike engine revving up, but Jack, embarking upon speech.

'We're expecting a bit of trouble. That's why we asked the Sergeant if he could help us out.'

'Trouble at an Art Exhibition?' Oliver repeated blankly. 'What sort of trouble? An attack by the militant wing of Art Critics Anonymous?'

'Something like that,' Sergeant Prendergast agreed, smoothly. 'There's quite a strong local movement—a sort of informal group supporting representational art, and not spending public money on—well—on things like this. But it's wonderful how the sight of a uniform calms them down,' said the Sergeant cheerfully. PC Oliver restrained himself from asking how he would know, after a long career devoted to keeping his uniform and its wearer well out of sight of possible trouble. But the Sergeant was still talking. 'And believe me, lad, this is one place where we don't need trouble.' He finished his tea with a noisy flourish, (without any untoward sugar build-up apparently). He handed the cup to his junior.

'Just take that back, will you lad, then we'll be on our way.'

PC Oliver obeyed. All the bikers seemed to be doing the same, finishing tea, handing back cups, (and putting any litter neatly into a bin in the shape of an open-mouthed pig thoughtfully supplied by the council—the joke policeman's helmet the creature was wearing was superglued to its head, as Oliver had discovered after a surreptitious attempt to tip it off) and preparing to mount and ride. It appeared that he was going to drive in convoy with them and indeed, he set off with a massive escort of bikers, riding in front, behind and to each side of the police car. He did not quite feel able to question the suitability of this situation with his superior officer, but he did just float the hopefully neutral comment: 'You seem to know a lot of these chaps, sir.'

'Yes,' said his Sergeant. 'Well, you know there's a vicar who's the bikers' padre. I reckon I'm the bikers' copper.' He sounded so complacent about it that Oliver did not like to question its suitability. There was one question, however.' I didn't think you—er—rode a bike, sir.'

'Too right I don't,' Sergeant Prendergast agreed with enthusiasm and after that there seemed very little to say. PC Oliver concentrated on not being distracted by the leather-clad thigh of Jack/Thorfinn's passenger which occasionally brushed his side window.

Eventually the convoy swept into the piazza in front of the town-hall which had been built in the fifties to replace a Gothic horror of a building, which had now become immensely fashionable, and been transformed into very expensive flats. Its replacement had a lot of tall white columns surmounted by a balcony of the sort from which uniformed dictators are seen pronouncing the beginning of a democratic republic (although it had only ever actually been used for the Mayor to introduce whichever fading soap star had consented to switch on the Winterval lights). The bikers parked their motorcycles in a tidy row, and strode up the steps of the town hall, followed by the two policemen.

The immense entrance hall was, apparently, the venue for the exhibition. The white walls were supplied with a number of floodlit niches, which may or may not have usually contained works of art of a more conventional kind but were currently empty. Jack/Thorfinn and several of his comrades hopped up into the niches and struck heroic poses in a cheerful kind of way. The others milled about the Hall, and were soon joined by the kind of thin, black-clad people who come to the opening of exhibitions of modern art, and a scattering of waitresses carrying trays of canapés and glasses of white wine. PC Oliver, who was not at all sure whether or not his presence was officially sanctioned, avoided the wine, but unbent so far as to eat a few canapés. Then he took up a position by the main doors and looked out for the trouble that Jack and Sergeant Prendergast appeared to expect. But perhaps the mere sight of his uniform really would defuse the situation.

After a while the audience stopped milling and gathered at the far end of the hall, where a platform had been set up, and a number of the thin, black-clad people embarked on a series of very dull speeches. PC Oliver understood that the pallid young man in a worn black sweater was the artist, while the red-faced man in the shiny navy suit was the head of the arts and culture department. They were just fulsomely congratulating each other on the exhibition when a small, incandescently angry man erupted from the crowd.

The words 'disgraceful . . . public money' and 'how can you call this art' were briefly audible and then, suddenly the hall was full of young men with short hair and rather square heads, wearing tee-shirts with the slogan 'CALL THIS ART?' who hurled themselves at the exhibits and tried to drag them from their niches. Not unnaturally they resisted. Their friends came to their support. And the sight of PC Oliver's uniform seemed to have no calming effect at all. Nevertheless he waded into the mob suggesting, loudly and uselessly that everyone calm down and remember that causing a breach of the peace was an arrestable offence . . . But all in vain. Mr Angry had managed to invade the platform and was making a sterling effort to choke the pallid young artist, who was defending himself with unexpected vigour. Sergeant Prendergast had, of course, vanished . . .

And then, quite unexpectedly he reappeared. He hurled himself at his junior officer, throwing him to the marble floor.

'What the . . .' PC Oliver gasped.

'Keep down lad,' his Sergeant roared. 'I hoped it wouldn't come to this, but it has.

Whatever you do, don't look at her.'

PC Oliver, of course, looked up instantly, in time to see Jack's lady beginning to remove her helmet. His Sergeant, acting with commendable and unexpected swiftness, pushed him back to the floor, but he had had time to see that the young woman had a head of the most remarkably thick and—lively—hair.

There was a sudden hush as the fighters became aware of what had happened on the platform. Sergeant Prendergast removed his grip from the back of PC Oliver's neck and he looked up cautiously. The young lady's helmet was back in place. And a new, remarkably ugly statue stood on the platform, depicting a small furious man in a suit attempting to throttle a young man in a sweater. The hall was emptying as bikers, art fanciers and others melted away, shaking their heads, and trying to deny the evidence of their own eyes.

'She turned them to stone,' PC Oliver whimpered. 'It's Medusa!'

'No, lad,' Sergeant Prendergast said. 'Medusa had her head cut off, if you'll remember. That's one of her sisters. Euryale she's called.'

'You can't have a gorgon biker!'

'Why not?' Practically the only way she can travel about—the snakes tuck nicely under the helmet and the smoked glass takes the edge of her Look. And naturally enough she's got an

59

interest in art—representational and modern . . .'

PC Oliver watched the slender young gorgon trip out of the hall with her companion. 'And I suppose that chap's Perseus,' he said, bitterly.

'Now, lad. Never use that name in her hearing. Those girls were fond of each other. No. That chap's had a lot of names. In England he's Jack—Jack the Giant Killer— you may have heard of him, but I doubt it, I don't know what they teach in schools these days, but back in the old days, in Greece he was called Herakles . . .'

*   *   *

The chimaera's voice died away and my mobile rang suddenly. I lunged for the phone. It was the agency I had visited that morning, offering me a job. When I had noted the details, and made myself another cup of celebratory tea, I said: 'What happened to the statue?'

'It was left on the platform for a while, until an eminent art critic came to look at it, and pronounced it 'too fantastic and lacking in any kind of reality' besides being very ugly. So it was donated to the local hospital.'

I looked at the chimaera.

It looked back at me, and, very gravely, winked.

THE SIXTH STORY

Late one beautiful summer evening I was sitting by the window in my high room, watching the last pinks and lavenders fade from the sky, and combing the wiry blonde mane of the chimaera who had taken up residence in my wardrobe. I was planning to use the combings to stitch the curls of the mane in a piece of embroidery depicting the little creature, but I was a little troubled by the fact that it seemed to be shedding rather a lot. When we first met it had told me it was possible that it would eventually dissipate into the air (quite painlessly) and I was concerned that this loss of fur might be the first stage in its dissolution. However, on the plus side, its compact little body which had at first been chill and cloud-like to the touch now felt quite firm, even muscular, and rather warm than otherwise.

When the last colour faded from the sky I put the lights on, made myself and the chimaera some lemon-balm tea, and took out my embroidery. I had just finished a satisfactorily long stretch on a film and banked a cheque from a commercial (which I had actually done before I met the chimaera, but that is—alas—the way commercial payments work) so I felt entitled to enjoy the few clear days that stretched ahead of me—provided of course that they didn't last too long. So I asked the chimaera to tell me one of its stories, perhaps one set in the film industry, but this time with a happy ending, that would suit the cosy atmosphere.

'Tell me a story about someone who really achieved their ambition,' I said.

It took a lap of its lemon tea, gave a little cough (perhaps to indicate the difficulty of the task I had set it) and embarked on a story called:

BUILDING UP HIS PART

'Heard about old Bob, then?' said the man who had just, inadvertently, elbowed Martin in the ribs in the scrum for coffee.

'No, what?' Martin seized two plastic cups and handed one to the man, to show he bore no malice for the elbow. An old lady nipped sharply in front of them both and began filling her cup from the urn.

'Gorn,' she said as she did so, 'shocking thing! And I was the last person to speak to him!' She might be dressed as a mummy but she still had the rich, plummy tones of the old-fashioned actress she must once have been, and her announcement was clearly audible for some yards around.

'Dreadful!' another lady of similar age but costumed as a hag, agreed vigorously. 'I was so shocked!'

There was a general murmur of shock and sympathy and the first old lady took advantage of the briefly subdued atmosphere to snag two of the rapidly decreasing stock of doughnuts and shuffle off.

'Beware the beat of bandaged feet,' said the man who had elbowed Martin, watching her flight. 'You get us some coffee, and I'll get the doughnuts.'

Martin darted forward to fill two cups, remembering, as he did so, that the man was called Jerry and they had worked together on *Fuzz*, an inexplicably popular police series, in which Martin had actually had a speaking part once. 'All right gov, you've got me bang to rights,' was the line, if he remembered correctly. Then he turned to fight his way back through the mob, which had resumed seething almost at once. Extras may come and extras may go, but coffee retains its essential importance. Martin made his way to a table and sat down with the coffee, next to Jerry and the doughnuts.

'How did it happen?' Martin asked. He had already begun to distance himself from the world of show business. His writing (he had just completed the first novel in a planned series of books about a dynasty of actors) was beginning to take off. He had not only found an agent, it actually looked as if his agent might have found him a publisher . . . but of course a potential publishing contract, however exciting, did nothing to pay the rent, and he had been quite grateful for the offer of a few days' background on a horror film. So now he sat sipping coffee with old Jerry, wearing the ragged suit and green complexion of the cinematic zombie. In the circumstances it seemed almost bad taste to be discussing Old Bob, but it seemed only polite to inquire.

'How did what?' Jerry asked through a mouthful of pastry.

'Bob. How did he die?'

'Oh, he didn't. Or at least if he did they never found the body. No, he vanished off the set of *Hunter's Moon* in the middle of a night-shoot.'

Hunter's Moon was the werewolf film whose unexpected success had spawned a number of imitations. In a way, Martin supposed, it had led to his being there that day. 'I never heard anything about that,' he said.

'Hushed up,' Jerry said, shaking his head. 'They searched all night. Well, they had the dogs there all ready.'

'Dogs?' Martin said blankly.

'They had half a dozen police-dogs playing the werewolves—moonlighting you could say,' Jerry added, chuckling.

Martin laughed dutifully.

'Well, they seemed quite pleased to have

some real work to do, and they combed the place—with their handlers—or they did once they'd been dragged away from the second lead's jacket.'

'Must have had a ham sandwich in his pocket,' said the mummy lady.

Martin and Jerry exchanged glances. 'Er—yes,' Jerry said, 'well, they didn't find anything. They got the local police in after a couple of hours, but they couldn't see that it was serious. All the sergeant did was drink coffee and finish up the doughnuts. He said Bob had probably just gone home. I mean, as if—Old Bob leaving a set before the wrap—it would have been the first time in history.'

'Yes,' Martin said, thoughtfully, remembering. It was true. Old Bob would never have voluntarily left a film-set until shooting was well and truly over.

Unlike many extras, Bob's ambition had been to get his face on camera as often as was humanly possible. Some, like Martin himself, with ambitions beyond the holding area, where the crowd was corralled when they were not needed, had been told that if they appeared too often in crowd scenes they would never be taken seriously by casting directors. Sometimes Martin did wonder who spent their time freeze-framing such scenes with the idea of exclaiming, 'Look, there's that Martin Taylor appearing as 'Passer-by' again. We certainly won't cast him . . .' but on the whole it was received wisdom, and he didn't argue with it. Others, the older ones who'd been in the profession for years, seemed to regard it as an affront to be asked to do anything other than attend for meals, drink endless cups of coffee and talk about the good old days.

But Bob wanted to work, and more importantly, he wanted to be seen working. He was remarkably, almost uncannily good at it, a legend amongst background artistes. He had acquired his own police uniform, as a young man, and thereafter appeared as more policeman than Martin had had hot dinners. But policemen were not his real triumph. Anyone, Bob suggested, could do the policeman bit. His talent was for turning up right next to the star. The bearded face that appears over the hero's shoulder at his moment of triumph in the first of a slew of sword and sandal epics belonged to Old Bob. The hand which takes the coats of the Golden Couple entering the nightclub at the climax of the retro comedy *Divorce Me Darling* (memorable only because shortly afterwards they did just that), was Old Bob's. The passer-by who hesitates for a moment outside the jeweller's during the heist in *Blague!* (one of last and weakest of the British gangster epics—so weak that unkind critics suggested that it had killed the genre and not a moment before time either) and very nearly gets shot by the nervous young look-out—was Old Bob.

66

'Of course,' Jerry continued, 'the crew knew he'd never have made off willingly. Everyone in the business knows Old Bob. But the police didn't. The most sensible suggestion they came up with was that he must have tripped over something, as anyone might on a set, hit his head, got disorientated and wandered off. Only if he had done he'd have been a bit noticeable, even at night, seeing as how he was in full werewolf make-up.'

Martin tried, and failed, to visualise even Old Bob cunningly disguised as a police dog. His puzzlement must have shown in his face because the mummy lady came in with an explanation.

'He was one of what they called the Transitionals—they had the Normals, the Transitionals who were very furry and had the teeth, just starting the change from man to wolf, you see, and then there were the police dogs. I was a Normal,' she added with a hint of pride.

Yes, Martin thought, he would have been difficult to miss. Unless—'Could there have been some kind of bizarre accident,' the writer in him suggested. 'Someone did see him prowling about, panicked, hit out, did him some fatal damage, then realised they'd killed a human, not a werewolf, and hid the body?'

'Possible, I suppose,' Jerry said, 'but it couldn't have happened all that far away, and if there was a murder-site and a fresh grave you'd have expected the dogs to find it. But it was funny that the dogs never picked up his scent—or rather they did, but they lost it just in front of B camera. It was as if he'd been snatched up into the air, someone said, but of course there was no way that could have happened.'

'And he never went back home?'

'No sign of it, if he did. They tried the hospitals, of course, they even dragged the canal, and they did what anyone who knew Old Bob would have tried first, they checked with all his agencies. Nothing. Zilch. And nothing since then either.'

'Wardrobe,' boomed the mummy lady, 'have never stopped moaning about losing those teeth.'

A nearby werewolf looked up. ''Ere! They don't recycle these fangs, do they?' he asked with some alarm.

'Not Old Bob's, certainly,' said the mummy lady with a grim chuckle.

'Well. There's a thing. Old Bob,' said Martin, 'he must have appeared in more films than any extra since 1890—do you remember that early film—*Confessions of an Undertaker*, wasn't it, where he walks down the path in a milkman's uniform, knocks at the door—and opens it to himself, as the householder in a dressing-gown?'

Martin and Jerry played 'do you remember' while they drank their coffee, dredging up more and more examples of Old Bob's ingenuity in getting in front of the camera, and, once there, building up his part. But then Jerry exclaimed, 'Look out!' He had spotted the AD, roving for prey. Instantly both men became very interested in the table top—'It's like a hostage situation,' Martin explained to friends. 'You avoid eye-contact . . .'—but in spite of that Jerry was borne away to the set. Martin turned his attention to the crossword in an abandoned newspaper until the neighbouring werewolf inveigled him into a conversation about football.

It was some weeks later that Martin happened to visit friends for a quiet evening involving a take-away, a supply of cheap wine and some videos. The female portion of the couple was a fan of one of the young actors in *Blague!* and, rather apologetically, she had included it in the evening's entertainment. Martin and the male partner talked amongst themselves while it was running . . . until the scene outside the jeweller's. Martin opened his mouth to draw attention to Old Bob. And then closed it again. Bob walked past the shop, then hesitated, according to the Director's instructions. There was some intercutting between Bob's anonymous, blundering passer-by and the sweaty, nervous youngster with the gun, hidden behind the window. There was some dramatic music. The crack of a gun. And Old Bob collapsed rather artistically onto the

69

pavement. The camera stayed on him for what must have been at least a minute of writhing and groaning, and—a final and rather effective touch—finished on a shot of one bloodstained hand crawling across the pavement, and abruptly becoming still.

'I don't remember that,' Martin said. But no one else saw anything odd and he forgot about it for a while. Until a moment of curiosity made him borrow a copy of *Divorce me Darling* from his local video library. He fast-forwarded it to the scene in the nightclub. He was not really surprised to see that now Old Bob had three lines and a really long close-up as he shook his head and smiled quizzically at the Golden Couple as if he knew just how their romance would end in real life.

The next day Martin had the fantastically good news he had been hoping for from the publisher and for a week he forgot about Old Bob. Then the worm of curiosity which must been working away at his subconscious, made him get out the Roman epic. Sure enough the camera slewed right away from the star and focussed entirely on Old Bob, who had, by this time, quite a long speech. Somehow Bob had got himself permanently into that world which had always fascinated him so much, (had he found a way in through B camera? Martin wondered wildly) and was happily involved in building up his parts. There seemed no reason why he should ever stop.

But the chimaera's soft little voice did stop. It lapped some more tea and said, smugly, 'There. Wasn't that a happy ending?'

'M'm. I'm not too sure about that. It seems rather spooky to me. Could you really vanish into a camera like that?'

'Of course,' said the chimaera. 'Haven't you ever heard of people being 'captured on camera'?'

'Or people whom the camera 'really loves', I said uneasily, suddenly detecting a rather sinister suggestion in this particular phrase. 'Did Old Bob ever escape?'

'He didn't want to. He finally got into *Gone with the Wind* and lived happily ever after.'

But I still thought it was spooky. Especially as I had worked with someone very like Old Bob at the beginning of the summer. He'd been on virtually every shoot . . . but recently I hadn't seen him anywhere. Not since *Hunter's Moon* anyway.

THE SEVENTH STORY

I had got into the habit of waking early that hot summer. Sometimes, of course, I *had* to wake early to get up and go to work at some far flung film-set, but when I had no work I could enjoy the bright, still hours before it became too hot, or I had become too twitchy because the phone was not ringing. Quite often I used the time to get on with my novel, but one morning, just before dawn, when the chimaera and I were sitting companionably on the old sofa watching the sky brighten and fill with delicate colour, it suggested that this would be a good time for a fairy story and I, looking at the magical sky, thought so too.

'But I think I have heard—or read—most of them,' I added.

'Ah. But I don't think you have heard one told quite like this,' it said firmly and began to tell the story of:

STRAW AND GOLD

It was very late when the dwarf came back to his little house in the depths of the Forest, so late that the night was almost turning into early morning. But as he stepped across his threshold a green fire sprang up in the hearth, and *she* rose up from her place beside the fire and danced towards him holding out her hands.

'You have come home,' *she* lilted in glad surprise.

He gazed at her. The room was lit silver and green, half by moonlight, and half by those strange flames, and by that light he could see that *she* was still the most exquisite creature he had ever made. Her fine hair was the soft pale gold of willow leaves in autumn, but now, and sometimes in bright sunshine, it had a greenish sheen. Her skin was as white as a peeled willow wand, she moved with a living willow's grace, and when she spoke her voice was sweet as falling water and soft as rustling leaves. Her eyes were the vivid green of spring willow, and now they glowed with pleasure at the sight of him. And *she* was not real. *She* danced, or walked or stood still, at his will and spoke the words he gave her. If it had suited his mood she would have shrilled at him, like the wives he had heard in the village, demanding to know where he had been and why he had kept her waiting, or whimpered that she had been afraid, alone in the dark Forest without his strong arms to protect her . . . he looked at her for another moment and then he spoke the Word of Unmaking, and she fell at his feet, collapsing into a little heap of woven willow branches, with a sound like a tiny sigh. So tiny that he could not tell if it had meant relief or regret.

He gathered up the branches, and almost threw them into the fire. But then he reminded himself they had been living things once, until he changed them for his pleasure, and he went outside. The longest branch he thrust into the soft damp earth, the rest he scattered on the grass. Then he went back into his little house to prepare for bed. He told himself that his

73

mood was only the natural sadness of the artist who has been forced to destroy a beautiful creation which has fallen short of his wishes, so that he might try again. But he knew he would not make another poppet like that one.

He woke still burdened by unhappiness he could not explain, so he made up his mind to throw it off. He would have a tea-party. These had always given him enormous, quiet pleasure. *They* were certainly real. He had seen pictures of such parties, painted on the walls of a royal nursery. They showed birds and animals, some decked out with bows and little collars round their necks, sitting round a toadstool table eating tiny cakes and drinking tea from tiny painted cups. In his experience, pictures were more often of stiff, ugly kings, and women in rich dresses at great feasts than of these charming little animals, but they were always true copies of the world. But this time when he sat in the afternoon sunshine, with his small furry guests he realised abruptly that this too was wrong. The animals were there under duress. It was his magic that was making them sit there so unnaturally still, clinging to cups with clumsy, unhappy little paws. No one—except for him—was *enjoying* it. And so *he* couldn't enjoy it any longer. He put down his pretty little cup, which faded out of existence even as he did so. Then he went back into his little house and shut the door. As he did so he thought, with a sudden pang that he should at least have given the rabbits a bit of a start before he freed the foxes.

But he had been living the Forest for a long, long time. Long enough for his changing magic to have changed the animals around his cottage to something—other. They were bigger and cleverer than the animals on the edge of the Forest. And they could talk to the dwarf—which he knew—and to each other, even when he was not there—which he did not. They had agreements about predation ('Don't eat anything that talks' for instance) and they talked now.

'He's sad,' said a rabbit.

'Perhaps,' a vixen suggested, 'he has lost a cub.'

'It must have been a long time ago, then,' said an otter.

'But he might remember sometimes,' a squirrel said. 'I lost a good store of nuts once, and now, even when I'm eating a really big chestnut I think of the store I lost and it spoils the flavour of the nut I've got—just for a moment.'

Several voices suggested that this was because the squirrel was, in fact, an idiot. His fellow squirrels proceeded to bring up other examples of his idiocy, including an alleged encounter with a garden ornament in the shape of a squirrel which could not have possibly have been true. The meeting threatened to break up in some disorder, until an elderly and much respected female rabbit drummed her feet in an alarm call and everyone fell silent.

'The dwarf is sad,' she said. 'But he has been kind to us.'

He had. Apart from his magic he had a great many practical abilities. He was clever with his hands, and knowledgeable about herbs, and there were few animals who had not benefited from his medical help at some time or another. He grew fruit and vegetables, far more than he needed for his small appetite, and he was generous with both. And he was gentle. They could appreciate gentleness, now they were clever.

'He likes tea-parties,' she said.

'But this one made him sad,' said a sparrow.

She nodded. 'Perhaps,' she said, slowly, 'it is because it has always been for *us*. Never for *him*.' She paused. 'We shall make one for him.'

Without the help of magic it would be a tremendous undertaking. But once the suggestion had been made it did sound like the right thing. They began, with a certain amount of excitement, to make a list of what they would need. There was a general agreement that the party should be a surprise, which meant that their preparations must be secret. This was made a good deal easier when the dwarf was called away by one of those mysterious messengers who came for him from time to time and went off, leaving his house shuttered and silent. He said goodbye to them kindly, but he still looked sad.

As soon as he was out of sight the planners broke into a frenzy of activity. The birds were sent out as scouts to identify the best source of supplies, and came back to say that the village was useless, but that there was a town a further flight away, where, on certain days, all sorts of goods were laid out on tables in the streets.

'And,' said one of the older birds, 'the people don't look up and they don't look down as a rule, they just peer straight ahead, so if you're quick and quiet they'll never see you helping yourselves.'

'But how are we to get there?' a squirrel protested.

It was one of the foxes, hanging about the outskirts of the village for his own purposes, who discovered the carrier's cart which set off early on market days to the town and came back, loaded down, late at night.

'A few of us could swing onto the back,' he said. 'Get to town, load up, and back the same day.'

'Load up into what?' said an otter.

'Baskets,' said the fox loftily. 'Bit like nests. The birds can make some.'

Some of the birds pointed out that they'd done their bit already with all that scouting, but others, who were rather proud of their nest-building were happy to demonstrate. The baskets were duly produced, neatly woven, and, as the birds pointed out smugly, really water-tight.

'Well, we're not going to carry soup in them,' a fox pointed out. 'And there's bits dropping off them already.'

'Only if you swing them about,' a crow said coldly.

In the end a chosen group of otters and foxes trotted off to the village, well before dawn, gripping the baskets carefully between their teeth, and *not* swinging them about. Only one was lost during the scramble into the cart, and none at all when they clambered out again and made their way to the market. A posse of birds had flown with them, and they flew ahead now to show the animals the way. Luckily it is impossible to argue about anything with a basket handle between your teeth, and they reached the market quickly, without problems.

There they discovered that the birds had been right. All sorts of things were laid out within paw-reach, and no one looked down to see what those paws were reaching for, except one child, who was slapped for lying when he drew attention to it. But while his mother was bargaining for a cabbage he saw the paw again, this time in conjunction with a pointy, whiskery face. The paw appeared to be beckoning. He wandered closer and it rammed something into his pocket and vanished. Warned by his previous experience he said nothing, but on later investigation he found his pocket had been filled with sweets. He ate them silently and with gratitude.

There were no further incidents. The raiding party returned, their baskets loaded with plunder, to find a sled made from branches waiting for them at the edge of the Forest. Everyone took turns to haul it back, and they put all the foodstuffs carefully inside the dwarf's house, where, they knew, they would remain safe and unspoiled. Things did, inside that house. There was, perhaps, something in the air.

The rabbit matriarch organised further teams to gather berries to be strung for decorations, or dried for a relish, herbs, also to be dried to make tea, and, from the rubbish heaps of wasteful and careless humans, any kind of domestic ware that could be used for cups and plates. Meanwhile she saw that the willow branch, which had taken root, and begun to grow into a pretty little sapling, was kept watered and protected. Somehow she felt this was the right thing to do.

*　　　*　　　*

The dwarf had gone to the King's court unwillingly enough. If he must feel sad, he thought, he would have rather have endured his sadness at home, cultivating his garden, wearing comfortable clothes and sleeping in his own small bed. Here he must wear a rich velvet gown, of a crimson so dark that until he turned and the folds caught the light it seemed black, embroidered with dull gold. He must wear tall boots, too, so that he could look the King's courtiers more or less in the eye, and he must sleep in a bed as large as his whole kitchen, draped with heavy curtains, lest a breath of air reach him. He must endure stares and whispers, and the knowledge that not so long ago as he reckoned time, the only role he would have had at court was to leap out of a pie at a banquet, as a figure of fun. They might have liked him better if he had been, but he was finely made, with a beautiful face and a body so well-proportioned that he made the tall courtiers look like lanky hobbledehoys.

They called him the King's alchemist, for they knew he made him gold, but for each supply of gold he exacted a promise, and though the King would willingly have done so he dared not break his promises, for if he did the gold would turn back into lead. And the King hated the promises because they bound him to give part of his gold to the poor and the sick, and never to use any of it to pay soldiers or to buy weapons. So he must build houses for the homeless and hospitals for the sick, and negotiate with his neighbours instead of fighting them. But he loved the gold too much to refuse it and he made the promises as he must and never realised that they made his kingdom richer and safer than ever the gold did.

But as yet the King had not asked for gold, and the dwarf did not know why he had been sent for. Sometimes Kings wanted advice, though they rarely took it, more often they wanted gold and that they certainly took. But all that had happened so far was that he had been ceremoniously introduced to the new young Queen. She was very young and very beautiful, almost as beautiful as his willow-girl had been, but the Queen's long golden hair was trapped in a golden net, and the white skin of her throat and breast was hidden by jewels. And her eyes were blue and very sad. Once she took him to the royal nursery to see her child, a little creature wailing in its gilded cradle as if it were as sad as she was. Perhaps, he thought, the Queen was sad because she knew that the courtiers called her 'The Miller's Daughter' because her father had been a rich merchant who had made his great wealth by buying up flour during a famine and selling it to the starving at a great price, and had no royal blood at all.

But one evening he came upon her sitting beside a fountain in the palace garden, letting her tears fall softly into the clear water. She gasped in surprise when she saw him, but she was wearing a silk gown as blue as the evening dusk, and a gold necklace like a spider's web, with great jewels caught in it here and there

81

that flashed and trembled as she sobbed like the wings of trapped dragonflies and he thought she had dressed to be discovered.

But he stood still and asked her why she was crying.

She lifted her blue eyes to him and said, 'Because I am going to die.'

'What do you mean? Are you ill? Or in danger?' he asked. But he felt as if he were reciting a part which she had written for him.

'No,' she said. 'But my husband is going to kill me.' She sobbed bitterly then while the jewels on her breast flashed still brighter. 'I was never presented at the Court. I stayed at home quietly with my father. But one day the King saw me sitting at my window, combing my hair, and he sent messengers to my father, offering to make me his mistress. Now my father was a dying man, and perhaps his wits were straying, or perhaps he wanted to do his best for me before he died, and what better could he do than make me a queen? But he told the King that I had been given a gift from my godmother, that I could spin straw into gold. But I could only do it for my lawful husband and only after I had been married to him for a year and a day. And so the King married me, and for all this year I have had all the jewels and the dresses and fine things that ever I wanted. But tomorrow morning they will put me into an attic room, with a spinning wheel and three trusses of straw, and if I cannot spin them into gold they will cut off my head in the market square.'

The dwarf nodded. The man had made a desperate gamble that his daughter would, in a year, make the King love her well enough to forget her strange dowry. Or that she might bear the King an heir . . . but her first child had been a girl. And the King had not forgotten the gold.

'You could help me,' the young queen said. 'You are so clever. What would three trusses of gold be to you?' She edged along the white marble seat, so that she could look up into his face.

The dwarf wondered if this was a plot of the King's, spun to get his gold without the inconvenience of a promise. But he said, 'And what will you give me for three trusses of gold?'

She looked at him under her long pale lashes, and unclasped her necklace. Now he could see the bare skin of her neck and breast glowing in the twilight. 'I could give you this,' she said. 'Or—this . . .' and she took the golden net from her head and the great silken mass of her hair fell down until its ends dabbled in the water.

'Or,' she stood up and stretched out her arms. 'If you do not want gold and jewels I could give you flesh and blood . . .'

Yes. He was sure she would stand, or dance, sing or speak at his word if he would do what she wanted. But it would not be real. For a moment he was minded to ask for that lonely scrap of a baby, but he did not, because he was afraid that she would say yes and prove how worthless she was.

'Keep your jewels,' he said. 'The gold is yours.'

And he turned on his heel and left her beside the fountain.

'But my husband must not know,' she called after him. 'It must be a secret.'

Yes,' he agreed, without looking back. 'A secret.'

It went as he had promised. Each morning he passed through the locked doors into her attic prison and took away a truss of straw, and each evening he brought back a truss of gold. And every day he saw the eyes of the King grow brighter. On the third evening he called the dwarf to his private chamber. Three trusses of gold lay on the table.

'I have no further use for an alchemist,' he said triumphantly. 'I shall never call you to visit my court again.' He spoke as if he thought the dwarf would be sorry for it. 'Now my wife can spin all the straw of the kingdom into gold for me.'

'And when she has done, you may thatch your cow houses with gold, but there will be little other use for it. For it will be as common as straw—but your farmers will not be able to bed their cattle in it,' the dwarf said carelessly.

The King looked, for a moment, as if the dwarf had struck him, but then his eyes grew cunning. 'I have enough for my needs,' he murmured, as if to himself, fingering the gold on the table. 'Enough for a life time. Rather than let it lose its value I shall strike off her right hand so that she can spin no more.'

'Do not do that,' the dwarf said. 'I can take her gift away, if you will.'

And the King, who never looked beyond the moment, nodded. So the dwarf spoke a word that meant nothing either bad or good, and left the chamber. Now he had been dismissed he was free of the bonds which had been laid on him more years ago than he could remember, to serve the kings of this country. He took off his court gown and his high boots, and went out into the night, in his shirt and breeches, and anyone who saw him go thought him one of the handsome page-boys who waited upon the nobles out on some errand of his own. He walked out of the city, and walked the long roads to his Forest, not caring much where he went, or what he did, except sometimes he wished he had asked for the baby, for it would have been company in his lonely cottage, and it would have been real.

*   *   *

The animals were pleased when squirrel scouts who had been stationed on the Forest edge reported that they had seen the dwarf on the road, coming towards them. It just gave them time to lay out the food they had plundered from the human market, and the berries, and nuts and fruits they had gathered from the Forest, to set out the bits of crockery they had found or stolen, and string the garlands of flowers and leaves between the trees. And to brush up the Present. (The squirrels, as they never stopped telling everyone else, had found the Present, and everyone agreed that it would be just the right thing, but it certainly needed a little tidying.) But by the time the dwarf, footsore and heartsore, had made his slow way to the depths of the Forest and arrived in the little glade in front of his cottage everything was ready.

It was then that they began to have doubts. Would the dwarf, who, after all, was used to visiting palaces, really like these heaps of cakes, not at their best after a long journey in those mud lined baskets? Or admire the garlands, which seemed to be wilting even as they looked at them? Or want to drink from a chipped cup stolen from a rubbish heap? When he did step into the clearing they were becoming so nervous that no one said anything. And the dwarf just stood still, gazing around him. A small otter, unable to endure the suspense called out 'Surprise!' and the adults followed suit.

'You did this—*yourselves*—for *me*?' the

dwarf said uncertainly. He was happy and surprised, and—oddly—shamed by their generosity, but none of his happiness showed in his face and voice.

Quite convinced that everything had gone badly wrong, the rabbit matriarch decided that it was time for the Present. The furry ranks opened and the Present tottered forward. He was not looking his best. Some of the ladies had done what they could to lick him a bit cleaner but there was little they could do with engrained dirt. And some of those marks, as they whispered to each other in horrified tones, were not dirt. They were bruises . . . burns. As he moved further into the clearing there were muttered explanations: 'The squirrels found him . . . in the middle of the Forest . . . they—his dam and her new mate brought him there and left him . . . wanted to get rid of him . . . we thought . . .'

The Present looked at the dwarf. He was much too young to be puzzled by talking animals. He had been surprised that they talked gently, calling him 'cubsy' and 'precious' and did not seem to know the words that had been hurled at him for most of his short life: 'brat' 'bastard' 'useless' but not that they *talked*. And he did not recognise any oddness in the dwarf at all. What he did recognise was a look he only remembered dimly, from the time when his father had been alive, a look he no longer hoped to see again. Kindness.

Gentleness. He stumbled forward and seized the dwarf's hand in his pudgy little paws.

'Dada?' he said.

It was the best party ever.

The dwarf was an excellent father. The little boy grew up strong and handsome, and eventually rescued a sad princess from her miserable palace home, and brought her to live happily the Forest. But that is another story.

The rabbit matriarch lived to a fabulous age, and spent much of her time sitting under the beautiful willow tree which now grew outside the cottage. She was expecting that, in the fullness of time, it would grow into another Present for the dwarf.

And she was right.

*   *   *

'I think I have heard that story before,' I said. 'But certainly not quite in the same way. In the version *I* know the dwarf is evil, and the miller's daughter rescues her baby by finding out his name.'

'I expect,' the chimaera said primly, 'that the king made *that* one up to explain to everyone why the dwarf didn't come back when he'd wasted those three trusses of gold. It didn't take him long.'

'Did the willow turn into a real girl?'

'Yes, she did. She and the dwarf got married and all the animals came to the wedding. And they lived happily ever after.'

I sighed, because so many fairy stories end like that and so few real life ones do. I felt that my novel was not going well and I was worried about my True Love. He regularly sent me excerpts from his travel diary, and sometimes I worried because he looked miserable, and unkempt and I was afraid he was not enjoying himself, and sometimes he looked happy and was surrounded by young and beautiful people and I was afraid he might be enjoying himself too much. So I went to my keyboard and put my heroine through a very nasty experience indeed.

The chimaera curled up and went to sleep in the sun.

THE EIGHTH STORY

One morning in the summer when I had a chimaera living in my wardrobe, I sat at my keyboard, determined to put in a good morning's work on my novel, and found I was quite unable to do so. I was waiting for the hob-man, and every sound set my nerves twitching. A week or so before I had decided that I was going to give a dinner party for various friends who had been through university with me, and who were now settled in nine-to-five jobs, and drifting into respectability. I wanted to give them a dazzling glimpse of *la vie bohème*, as lived in my attic, and at the same time prove that I was not forced to live on beans and toast, as they had so unkindly suggested. However, my hob had been gradually losing the will to live over the past few months, and was now down to one viable gas-ring—and while it may be *possible* to stun a group of friends with your cooking skills while using only one gas-ring I was not prepared to try it.

After a series of attempts to contact my landlord, involving, on my part, telephone messages left at various times of the day and night pleading for a visit, and, on his, notes, usually written in blue biro on small pieces of ruled paper, stating, untruthfully, 'I caled by you was out', we had finally achieved a meeting, which had resulted in a promise that today the hob-man (a friend, or, possibly and more worryingly, a relative, of the land-lord,) would arrive to set everything right. But now I was twitching helplessly, fearing that a phone-call from an agency, usually so urgently desired, would drag me away to a casting I could not miss, or that the hob-man would call himself and pronounce himself unable to turn up. To make matters worse there had already been two phone-calls, both from friends, in offices, who seemed to have plenty of time for telephone conversations. After the second one I abandoned my unfortunate heroine in a rather desperate situation, shut off my computer, and went to sit on the sofa for a good twitch. The chimaera joined me, and rubbed its head against my arm.

'I could tell you a story about someone who had real trouble with a hob. It might take your mind off things,' it offered.

I seized on the suggestion with real gratitude, and it began:

TROUBLE WITH THE HOB

PC Oliver tripped over a cable, blundered into a camera and, remembering in time the presence of three wide-eyed moppets, exclaimed 'Drat!'

The three moppets, hearing a swear word the like of which they had never heard before, simultaneously exclaimed 'OOOH!'

'What does that mean, mister?' inquired the largest of them.

'It means God Rot It,' Sergeant Prendergast explained with heavy kindness. 'But you mustn't say it. Only old ladies in Whitehall farces say drat these days.'

'What's a Whitehall farce, mister?' asked the smallest one.

'Is he an old lady then, mister?' asked the middle-sized one.

'A funny play, performed in a theatre by

real live actors, which you will never have seen, and never will see, very likely. And sometimes he might as well be.'

The moppets' mother bustled in with a tray of tea.

'Two sugars, wasn't it Sergeant Prendergast? And I thought you'd like some choccy biscuits.'

'Very kind, madam.' The sergeant was enthroned in the one free armchair in a sitting room otherwise cluttered with the kind of equipment required for outside broadcasting. His sidekick, PC Oliver was hovering (suitably enough) on the sidelines, trying to find somewhere where he wasn't in someone's way. The mother, taking pity on him, ruthlessly cleared another chair for him and sat him down with his mug of tea.

'When does the show usually start?' the cameraman inquired, accepting his mug.

She sighed. 'It's hard to say. It should be well under way by now, but—well—cameras do seem to put him off.'

'Charlie doesn't like cameras,' the smallest moppet pronounced oracularly.

'Charlie,' said a man who had been standing silently in a corner, taking notes and austerely refusing tea. 'Why do you call him Charlie?'

'It's his name,' said the moppet in the tone of someone who didn't do silly questions. 'What's *your* name?'

The man unbent slightly. 'I'm called Charlie

92

as well,' he said. 'After Charles Fort. What are you called?'

'Maximilian Terentius Albus,' said the moppet.

There was a sudden silence, broken by the sound of a large man choking on a chocolate biscuit.

'He's obsessed by Roman history,' his mother said apologetically. 'You see his father and I agreed that they could choose their names when they were old enough. We used to call him Piggy,' she added.

'I'm Princess Barbie Xena,' said the middle-sized one. PC Oliver rather thought, looking at the mother's fixed smile, that their parents had expected their children to choose more sensible names, Darwin, perhaps, or Florence Nightingale Emmeline Pankhurst.

'Did Charlie choose his name?' asked the man with the clipboard.

The three children looked at each other and shrugged.

'I think,' the mother said, hesitantly, 'it came from one of the newspaper reporters.'

The man could be seen crossing something out on the clipboard with rather more force than might have seemed strictly necessary.

'I mean,' she continued, 'he doesn't actually talk as such—he just—throws things about.'

'But you do seem to identify it as 'he',' said the man with the clipboard.

'Well, I suppose it's because he makes so

much mess,' she said. The men in the room looked self-conscious, but Princess Barbie Xena giggled.

'Well, there's not much happening at the moment,' said the cameraman. 'Mind if I nip out for a ciggie?'

'You go ahead,' Sergeant Prendergast said expansively. 'Young Oliver here will come and fetch you if there are any manifestations.'

PC Oliver reflected bitterly that he might have expected to end up on poltergeist-watch with this sergeant. Obviously the authorities had noticed Prendergast's uncanny affinity with the supernatural. There was that business with the moon goddess turning a burglar into a stag, and the gorgon at the art exhibition, to say nothing of the incident of the missing actor, when he and the sergeant had been dragged out to a film-set in the middle of the night to interview a lot of actors dressed up as werewolves (or, at least, he hoped they had been actors—with Prendergast you just couldn't be sure), and now, here he was, co-opted as the 'police presence' in the notorious Acacia Avenue Poltergeist Case.

'Of course,' the sergeant had said, 'it'll be the kiddies. It always is the kiddies in poltergeist cases.'

'But could children have shifted the fridge right across the kitchen?'

'You know how the press exaggerates.'

'There's a photograph,' Oliver had said

94

firmly.

There was a whole series of photographs. The entire inner section of the local paper had been devoted to photographs of the chaos the Acacia Avenue Polt had wrought in the kitchen of what had been a rather nice three-bedroom semi. In one picture the fridge was clearly seen to have been torn from its place and hurled across the room, blocking the kitchen door. Indeed, if human agency had been responsible it would inevitably have trapped itself inside the kitchen.

Sergeant Prendergast peered at the grey newsprint. 'Ah,' he said. 'Well, it's amazing how easy it is to move even the heaviest piece of furniture if you can just manhandle it onto a rug. Then you pull the rug, and it slides across the room. And as for getting out—that's where kiddies would have the advantage—they could wriggle through that gap, there,' and he indicated a gap (perfectly invisible to PC Oliver) with one thick forefinger.

PC Oliver did not feel equal to further argument, although he was rather surprised to find his superior officer arguing against a supernatural explanation. He had appeared to accept the moon-goddess and the gorgon only too easily.

So now they were waiting in the sitting room (partly because the presence of spectators put Charlie off, partly so that the children could be completely cleared of any

95

complicity in producing the special effects if and when they arrived). Sergeant Prendergast was not the only one to connect poltergeist activity with children, although one of the psychic experts the newspapers had consulted insisted: 'It often happens that the initial manifestations are perfectly genuine but they tend to peak and then die off. If they are under investigation at the time then the children often tend to feel under some kind of obligation to supply more—events.'

Their mother certainly seemed to think it was necessary to apologise for Charlie's lack of activity.

'I'm really sorry,' she said helplessly. 'I mean, some nights he simply goes wild. You'd almost think that he knows you're here and he's sulking.'

The words were hardly out of her mouth when there was a most appalling crash from the kitchen.

'Strewth!' Sergeant Prendergast said. 'That sounded as if it's broken every dish in the dresser.'

'That's probably just what he has done,' the lady said resignedly.

'Quick, Oliver, you run for the camera chap,' the sergeant said. 'Tell him things have started up again.'

But the cameraman had heard the noise too, and was legging it back down the garden path. He picked up his camera, and directed it through the serving hatch which PC Oliver helpfully opened for him. They waited breathlessly.

'Can you see anything?' Princess Barbie Xena inquired.

'Lot of broken dishes,' he said. 'No—wait—there! I could swear I saw something dart across the floor! It looked sort of—hairy. Have you got a cat? 'Or a ferret?'

The lady shook her head. 'No. Nothing like that.'

'That was Charlie,' Maximilian etc announced. 'He's hairy. And he darts.'

'Does he indeed?' Sergeant Prendergast heaved himself to his feet. 'Would I be right in thinking, madam that you did, once, have a cat?'

She looked blank. 'Yes, we did. But Princess seemed to be a bit chesty and I thought she might be allergic, so we gave Fluffy to my mother. He always liked her more than us, anyway,' she added with a faint touch of bitterness.

'And—I'm guessing here, but I would say that at around the same time as Fluffy left you, you obtained a dish-washing machine?'

'Why—yes—we had a small win—I think it was the Premium Bonds, but it could have been the Lottery—somehow we *do* seem to be lucky . . . so we treated ourselves. But however did you guess that?'

'And when the dishwasher was fitted you

started to get poltergeist trouble?'

She sat down in his vacated chair. 'Yes. Yes. But how . . .?'

'Because it all hangs together. You haven't got a poltergeist, madam. You've got trouble with your hob.'

'With the stove . . .' she repeated.

'No, no, madam, with your hob. Or Hob-goblin. It's a sort of hairy household spirit. Some people call it a brownie, some a billy-blind, but it all means the same thing. They keep the kitchen clean, wash dishes, bring a bit of domestic luck—small lottery wins, that sort of thing, but they like you to spend the money on the house, of course. They don't expect much in return—never, never, thank them, and never offer them clothes, but the odd saucer of milk doesn't come amiss. I'd be willing to bet that Fluffy was sharing his saucer with a hob.'

'Drat!' said the man with the clipboard. 'Another waste of an evening.' He sat down glumly. 'I sometimes wonder if I'll ever find a genuine poltergeist.'

'In my experience,' Sergeant Prendergast said, heavily, 'it's usually the kiddies.'

The cameraman gave a sharp exclamation. 'I've got him in focus. A sort of naked hairy little man—oh—f—rats! we can't use that!' He turned a rather red face from his camera.

'Realised that you were filming did, he?' the Sergeant asked.

'I think he must have done. He did something quite unnecessary that we certainly can't put out before the watershed.'

'Don't worry lad. I don't think he'll show up on film anyway.'

'Can we make him go away?' the lady asked plaintively.

'Yes. Make him a little suit of clothes and he'll be off faster than you can say 'knife'. But think about it. Has this been a happy house up till now?'

'Oh—yes. Until—this—happened. Everyone said it had a really lovely atmosphere. We felt it at once, it's why we bought it.'

'And you've had little pieces of luck you say—on and off?'

She thought about this. And nodded.

'Worth a few saucers of milk, wouldn't you say? Oh, and getting rid of the dishwasher.'

'Why on earth . . .?'

'Because they like to be kept busy. Known for it. They used to undo the work that had been done during the day, and do the work that had been left. Leave him some dishes to wash, and a saucer of milk, and he'll quiet down in no time. Oh, and I'll go and give him a bit of a talking to before we go.'

'Oh, would you . . .'

Sergeant Prendergast strode ponderously off towards the kitchen. They heard the rumble of his voice, interrupted by silences that were—somehow—rather eloquent. They began as impertinent, modulated to self-justifying and finished as rather penitent. Finally speech was replaced by the unmistakeable sound of a dustpan and brush being used to sweep up rather a lot of broken crockery. Sergeant Prendergast strode back.

'He's tidying up. He likes gold-top he says, with a drop of cream on high-days and holidays—of which there are quite a few in the hob calendar, I have to say—and—and this is rather important—he'd much rather not be called Charlie.'

*   *   *

'And that,' the chimaera concluded, 'was the end of the Acacia Avenue Poltergeist Case.'

'Did the poor lady have to get rid of her dish-washer?'

'No. She taught the hob how to load it. He became very interested in technology, and started to spend quite a long time on the internet, during the hours of darkness, chatting with hobs around the world.'

I was going to ask about this worldwide hob-community because I had always thought of hobs as being rather insular, very British creatures. But at that very moment the hob-man knocked on the door, and I barely had time to cover the chimaera with a cushion (the landlord was quite intransigent on the subject of pets) and rush to open it, before he could

drop one of those little notes through the door
and get away.

THE NINTH STORY

My supper party went very well. It could have
been my imagination, but it seemed to me that
the chimaera, although it did not put in an
appearance, diffused a pleasant atmosphere
throughout the flat, and then, everyone
seemed to enjoy watching some selected
footage of My True Love's travels, and there
was general agreement that it would make a
most excellent television documentary. Indeed,
everything would have been very pleasant if
only the weather had not been so hot. And I
had not still been concerned about the way the
chimaera seemed to be moulting—its mane,
in some lights, was almost invisible. And I
occasionally thought its tail was changing
too—becoming shorter and altogether less
scaly . . . and there was something about its
front hooves. I did not, of course, to look too
closely, but I worried.

A hot June turned into a burning July and
I had three days' work on a film that—as so
very often happens in the film world—was set
in December in an airport which meant the
crowd had to wear heavy coats and boots. On
the last evening I barely had the energy to drag

myself home, and even after a cold shower and a long drink of iced lemonade all I could do was lie on the cool floor boards and beg the chimaera to tell me a story that would really make my blood run cold.

'Well,' it said a little dubiously, 'I will do my best. Perhaps you would like to turn out the lights.'

I did so. The room was not really dark of course, as it was lit by that purple-orange glow that always burns in the night sky above London. Now I was on my feet I decided to sit beside the open window with another iced drink—it seemed more polite to listen to a story sitting up than sprawling on the floor, however cool it might be. The chimaera sat beside me.

'I will stop if it gets too scary,' it assured me, and then began:

RUBIES AND DIAMONDS

The Very Rich Old Man caused a great deal of trouble at the hotel even before he arrived. From the early morning the hotel manager had been fussing about, seeing that his suite was arranged in accordance with his very specific instructions, and all the staff who had been chosen to wait upon him were ready for the minutest inspection. And then, of course, the

Very Rich Old Man was late, so late that the manager could have let his suite three times over while they waited for him. So, long after the young assistant hall-porter should have gone off duty he was kept hanging about in the lobby, waiting for the Very Rich Old Man.

He complained, though quietly, that he might as well have stayed in his home village, and joined the army like all the other young men. He added, less quietly, that he had, after all, run away from home to avoid this kind of parade, and he was sure that the Emperor himself did not keep his troops waiting about like this. No one paid any attention to him, except the old head-porter, who promised him a taste of military discipline that he would not forget in a hurry, as soon as their important guest was settled in. And the young assistant hall-porter said that he was probably not coming anyway. He had probably dropped dead on the road from old age. Upon which the great double doors of the hotel were thrown open and the Very Rich Old Man came in.

And the young assistant hall-porter was forced to admit, though only to himself, that the guest would have been impressive even if he had been a Very Poor Old Man. He had the kind of face, the young man thought, that you saw on old coins. His profile was clean and clear-cut, and he had marvellous silvery hair, brushed back from his forehead, a high hawk nose and piercing black eyes. And the young man found himself hoping that his uniform was in a fit state to stand inspection from those dark eyes as the man moved down the line of bowing and curtseying hotel staff. It was not until he was safely past that the young man realised that he had not come alone. Walking behind him was a small figure, muffled in a fur cloak, and he supposed at first that she must be the old wife of the Very Rich Old Man, because all he could see of her was a glimpse of white hair peeping over the high collar of the cloak. But then the housekeeper bustled forward to take the cloak, and when she whisked it off her shoulders there was a transformation: the hair that was piled so elaborately was white as spun sugar, but it was the hair of a young blonde girl.

She was so tiny and delicate that she might have been a decoration on one of the elaborate cakes for which the hotel was so famous. She was dressed in a full-skirted gown of yellow silk, that was sashed very tightly around her tiny waist, and fitted very closely about the bodice, and it whispered as she walked across the polished parquet, and the young man thought it looked much more like a ball-gown than the kind of dress that ladies usually wore for travelling. The neck was so low that he could see the tops of her creamy breasts. And round her soft white throat had been tied a broad ribbon of gold coloured velvet. Now the young assistant hall-porter was a very respectable young man indeed, and never went to visit the young ladies in Paradise Alley, even on the Emperor's birthday when such an indulgence was almost a patriotic duty.

But as this lady drifted past him he had a sudden wish to lean forward and tug the end of that ribbon with his teeth, and watch it unroll across her bosom. And just as he formulated this shocking idea the young lady turned to look at him, and she saw that her eyes were as blue as an angel's and he found himself blushing hotly, with pure shame. Then, to make matters worse the young lady hurried forward and put her little white hand on the arm of the Very Rich Old Man, and murmured something that made him glance round at the young assistant hall-porter with no very pleasant expression, though no doubt it was the expensive gas-lights of the lobby which gave his eyes such a reddish gleam. But the hotel manager had come forward to escort his guests up the wide stairway, and he was not going to be delayed by anything as insignificant as an assistant hall-porter. So the couple vanished round the golden curve of the banisters and the hotel staff who remained in the lobby relaxed a little.

'Is that beautiful young lady the Old Man's daughter or his grand-daughter?' asked the assistant hall-porter innocently.

'Neither the one nor the other,' said the old

head-porter shortly, 'she's his wife. That's the kind of wife you get when you're as rich as he is, my boy.'

And one of the waiters joked that they had better have a doctor on hand because a night with a gorgeous piece like that would probably finish such an Old Man off completely, and the assistant hall-porter, who up until then, apart from the occasional murmur about discipline, had been a very quiet and well-behaved young man, hit the waiter on the nose. A moment later they were fighting all over the lobby, to the serious detriment of the long lace curtain and the potted plants.

They were very quickly pulled apart, and there was a general feeling that the fight was rather a welcome release from the day's tension. Both combatants were fined for the damage they had done to their respective uniforms, and made to clear up the lobby under the unforgiving gaze of the old hall-porter, but nothing worse was proposed. Indeed they went off together arm in arm and spent the rest of the night drinking beer in a student tavern, and lamenting the fact that they were not themselves Very Rich Old Men, and married to someone who must be the most beautiful woman in the Empire.

So the assistant hall-porter returned for his next period of duty feeling more than a little fragile. The old hall-porter looked at him sourly, and told him that the wife of the

Very Rich Old Man had made a number of purchases that day which had been delivered to the hotel, and now had to be taken up to their suite.

'So there's a job for you, my boy,' he said. 'Take that lot upstairs. And—watch yourself.'

And the young assistant, conscious of his recent misbehaviour ducked his head, and said he would. But, also conscious of months of previous good behaviour he added that he was not, after all, likely to start a fight in the actual presence of a guest.

'That's as maybe,' said the old hall-porter. 'But—that stuff's been lying about down here all afternoon. The gracious lady waited for you to come on duty before she asked for it to be brought up.'

'Why would she do that?' said the young assistant hall-porter nervously.

But the old head-porter only muttered that 'she was the cat's grand-mother' and his young assistant devoted himself to the task of carrying the gracious lady's parcels and packages up the service stairs, until they were all assembled outside the door of the Very Rich Old Man's suite. When he was making his last trip he came across one of the chambermaids on the landing, her apron thrown over her head, sobbing violently, and when he asked her what was wrong she only pushed past him, and ran down the stairs.

Then, with considerable misgivings, he

prepared to knock on the door. Had the young lady somehow read his thoughts about her bosom? Had she merely seen him looking at her bosom? Should he, perhaps, run away and join the army after all? But even as he hesitated an imperious voice from within said 'Enter!' and he opened the door and began to carry in the parcels.

The suite was very brightly lit by the hotel's famous gaslights, but the windows were tightly curtained. And the young man stood still in horror, because the beautiful young lady was sitting curled up in an armchair and she was wearing what could only be a dressing gown. It was made of dull crimson velvet, and the top half was like a military jacket, with black frogging, and a high stiff collar so he could not see her breasts and her throat at all. But he knew that they were there, covered only, perhaps, by the thin lawn of her nightdress. And her pale, pale hair was loose, the long curls streaming over her shoulders, right down almost to the hem of the full skirt of her dressing gown. For a moment all he could think of was what his grand-mother would have said about a young lady who would sit with her hair down, and her stays off while a strange young man came into the room. And the sweat broke out on his forehead. But the young lady waved her hand, indicating that he should bring the packages in, and the Very Rich Old Man, who had been lying on the sofa, reading aloud, went on reading aloud, in a foreign language that the young man could not understand. So he brought the packages inside, being very careful not to look at the young lady, and piled them against the wall. The young lady raised her hand with a rainbow flash of rings to half-conceal a wide pink yawn.

'That is such a tiresome story,' she said.

'I'm sorry my dear,' said the Very Rich Old Man. 'I thought it was rather apt.'

'A *very* tiresome story,' repeated the beautiful young lady. 'I want to look at everything I bought today. Tell the young man to open the parcels.'

And the Very Rich Old Man turned almost apologetically to the young assistant hall-porter, and told him to open the parcels, and the young man, his ears burning, unknotted string, and unwrapped paper, and opened boxes. The beautiful young lady snatched out dresses of lace, and silk, and satin and velvet, in colours of scarlet, and rose, and dark purple and black, and matching velvet cloaks from the bigger boxes, and bracelets and necklaces of brilliant stones from the smaller packages, and held them against her while she flounced about the room admiring them, and calling on the Very Rich Old Man to tell her how well they became her. But she never looked in the mirror, and the young assistant hall-porter realised that this was because there were no mirrors there. All the mirrors had been taken away from the suite, even the one over the mantelpiece which had been fastened to the wall. He could see the big rectangle of wallpaper it had covered, and the holes at each corner. And he gathered up the string, and the wrapping paper and the boxes as quickly as he could, and he bowed to the Very Rich Old Man, and the Beautiful Young Lady, and hurried out of the room.

He went back to the lobby, where the old head-porter took one look at his face, and hurried him into a back room, where he gave him a glass of plum-brandy. But when the young man tried to tell him what had frightened him so badly he would not listen to him. And after a while they went back to the lobby, and the young assistant hall-porter thought he would try to slip out of the hotel door and lose himself in the streets. But every time he tried the old head-porter was between him and the door. No guests came in to distract them, but they spent the whole evening playing a wretched game of Grand-Mother's Footsteps, and the old head-porter was much too sharp to be caught out. So the young man was still in the lobby when the golden clock that hung above the great desk struck twelve.

And at that moment the Very Rich Old Man came down the stairs with the beautiful young lady on his arm. She was wearing one of her new dresses, a ball-gown with great sweeping skirts and a close-fitting bodice of black lace. Her hair was dressed with ivory combs set with diamonds, chains of diamonds spiraled up her bare arms almost to the shoulders, and a there was a broad collar of diamonds round her throat. The Very Rich Old Man led her into the ballroom, and the young assistant hall-porter followed them and the head-porter did not try to hold him back.

The ball-room had been decorated with great swathes of red and black silk, which cascaded over the mirrors that lined the walls, and all the vases were filled with red lilies, and the room was lit by three blazing gasoliers. It was all ready for a grand ball, but there were no dancers, and there was no orchestra to play for them, but as soon as the Very Rich Old Man led his wife into the middle of the empty floor a waltz began to play, out of the air, and it was music that made the hairs stand up on the back of the young assistant hall-porter's neck. The beautiful young lady swept a magnificent curtsey and the Very Rich Old Man bowed almost to the ground, and then they began to dance. And as they danced the young man saw a very strange thing: the beautiful young lady's diamonds began to take on a faint colour, a delicate cloudy pink at first like a glass of water with a tiny drop of red wine in it, then they grew red, then blazing scarlet, so when at last the waltz came to an end she was wound and crowned with rubies. And when the music stopped the Very Rich Old Man dropped down white and bloodless in the middle of the ballroom floor, and she laughed aloud and held out her redly glistening arms to the young assistant hall-porter and shrieked aloud: 'Dance with me now, young man! For I need a fresh partner!'

And he ran out of the ballroom, and through the lobby of the hotel, and through the city streets, until he came to the barracks, where he enlisted for active service in the army, and never came back to the city.

*   *   *

There was a small silence and then the chimaera asked, hopefully, 'Was that chilling?'

'It was. There are goose pimples on my arms,' I assured it, although they may have come from the slight breeze from the window. 'What happened to the young man?'

'He made a success of his army career, and went back to his village at last for a long and happy retirement. But for the rest of his long life he wondered what would have happened if he had danced with the beautiful young lady.'

There was another pause.

'What would have happened?' I asked.

The chimaera shook his head. '*Much* too scary,' it said firmly.

And perhaps it was right.

THE TENTH STORY

It was late August and I was getting ready to go out to a party. It was going to be partly in the woods (and you may not think so, but it is quite possible to find woods in London) and partly on someone's allotment, where we would have a bonfire and toasted snacks. We had been asked to wear costumes with the theme of *A Midsummer Night's Dream*. While I put together something that would look suitably fairy-like, but at the same time be ready for anything the woods could throw at it the chimaera sat on its cushion, watching me with its round amber eyes, making the occasional helpful suggestion and admiring comment.

I felt a little guilty about leaving it alone, while I was going out to enjoy myself. I had indeed offered to smuggle it into the festivities in a shopping bag, so that it could emerge when the party had reached the stage where the appearance of a chimaera would cause no surprise at all, but it assured me that it would be quite happy at home. I had recently acquired a digital radio, and it had quickly learned how to use it, employing both its small hooves and its tail to tune it to the station he wanted. It was, it assured me, looking forward to an evening spent listening to Stories. But, it hastened to reassure me politely, it was sure it would have enjoyed the party as well. And while I added judicious amounts of glitter to my face, and pinned flowers in my hair, it told me one of its own stories, about another Midsummer festivity:

THE TUMP

PC Oliver struggled through the rainy darkness, following as best he could, in the large and flat footsteps of his superior officer. Abruptly he missed his footing, and found himself in a sitting position, performing a spectacular glissade down the side of the grassy hill he had just been climbing *up*.

'Come *on* Oliver,' Sergeant Prendergast called from the darkness above him. 'Stop acting the fool, man. We're supposed to be protecting the Tump from that sort of thing.'

'Yes, Sergeant,' Oliver said, spitting out bits of grass and mud which had somehow got into his mouth on his downward journey. 'But do we have to do it from the top? Wouldn't be better at the *foot* where we could stop people climbing up?'

'Not unless you want to keep running round and round it—and then you might miss one. Whereas if we're at the top we can see them as they attempt to ascend.'

'And shout—"Stop, in the name of the law?"' Oliver demanded with some bitterness.

'Whatever floats your boat, lad,' the Sergeant agreed imperturbably.

Oliver reached the top of the mound and flattened himself on the wet grass. 'Suppose,' he asked hesitantly, 'they *don't* stop?'

'Then you and I will have to *stop* them, won't we? And we won't do it from the prone position will we?'

Oliver wondered whether to risk asking if he wasn't actually *supine*, but he was by no means sure of his facts, and decided against it. Instead he hauled himself cautiously into a standing position. A sudden gust of wind hurled bitterly cold rain into his face. It felt *deliberate*. 'Remind me of why we're here,' he said.

'Because it's Midsummer Day,' Sergeant Prendergast informed him. 'Or it will be shortly. And we are here to stop an ancient, nay, prehistoric, monument named—with a certain lack of imagination, the Tump— or it has been for a couple of centuries, our Victorian ancestors having taken exception to its original name of Tit's Tump on the grounds of it sounding a bit rude—to stop it being used by persons of the hippie and pagan persuasion for unlawful ceremonies which could damage its surface. And talking of damage, I hope your thermos flask didn't get broken in your previous descent.'

Activated by this very heavy hint, Oliver produced a thermos from inside his jacket and poured his superior officer a cup of hot, sweet tea. 'But I mean to say,' he protested as he handed it over, 'the Tump's been here for a long time without a police guard and it seems to have avoided too much damage.'

Sergeant Prendergast took a long swallow of hot tea, and pointedly averted his eyes from the trail of mud and flattened grass that PC Oliver had left during his descent. 'Well, more or less perhaps. But that was before it was designated as an Ancient Monument and a National Treasure.'

Oliver peered down at the wet grass. 'It looks a bit like a—a sort of lump of earth to me,' he said. 'I mean, who *says* it's a prehistoric mound?'

'An eccentric Victorian gentleman,' said his Sergeant, 'a Doctor Royston who made up his mind that King Arthur was buried inside it.'

'King Arthur,' PC Oliver said, through clenched teeth, 'wasn't prehistoric.'

'He was never buried, either. As his biographer Thomas Malory put it, "in this world, he *changed his life*" and went off for a kind of holiday in Avalon. The Isle of Apples. Very nice place, I believe. Bit like Centre Parcs, but *quieter* I've always fancied.'

PC Oliver found himself visited by a surprisingly vivid mental picture of King Arthur, a rather doleful, moustachioed figure, dressed in a peculiarly Victorian version of medieval chain mail bicycling slowly through the morning mist along a tree lined avenue. A fishing rod was strapped to the bicycle, and there was a packet of sandwiches and a primitive thermos in the basket attached to the handlebars. He shook his head to get rid of the vision, and gritted, 'So, King Arthur's definitely not under there, and we've only got a loony Victorian's say-so that it's prehistoric at all . . .'

'Now, I didn't say that, lad. It could well be. It's been here for a while, that we do know. We've got records. The Reverend Thaddeus Jerningham tried to dig it up in the seventeenth century.'

'Who was he—another Victorian loony?'

'*Seventeenth century* lad,' the Sergeant corrected ponderously. 'He was the local Vicar, and very much of the Puritan persuasion. He said it was a High Place and a den of Iniquity and Idolatry and he took exception to his parishioners dancing round it on Midsummer Day, although they called it St John's Eve then. He had a particular dislike of morris dancers, apparently. 'For what are their bells but a tinkling summons to Satan's service . . .' that's one of his more repeatable pronouncements. He didn't approve of St John, of course, or dancing—or anything much as far as I can see, but he said this particular celebration was a great cause of fornication,

117

the birthing of bastards, and the de-virgination of the maids of the parish.'

'Not really the way you'd expect a clergyman to talk . . .' Oliver said weakly.

'They did tend to call a spade a spade in those days, lad. There was a bit of a protest about his language from some of the ladies, but he said he was surprised they should blush to hear named by daylight that which they had no scruple to do in the dark. And that was the end of that.'

'Why didn't he dig the Tump up, then?' PC Oliver's tone suggested that he felt the reverend gentleman had been a bit remiss there.

'The first time he set his spade to it something made him look round and he saw his house was on fire. So he rushed off to put it out, but when he got there—no fire. So he went back to the mound, and there was no sign of his spadework, but he started to dig again . . . and the same thing happened. And the third time he came back to the mound, and really dug into it, and took no notice of what he now thought was a delusion . . . until he heard his wife screaming, and realised his thatch really was on fire, and by the time he got back that time the house was pretty well lost.'

'Yeah, right,' Oliver said unpleasantly.

'Upon which,' the Sergeant continued, '*he* lorst it. Or so his parishioners thought. He was seen, over the next few weeks, wandering about the Tump 'in the dark of the moon' talking to himself. Or at least they *hoped* it was to himself. And one night, according to his long-suffering wife—she was called Kerenhappuch, which in my opinion was not the least of her problems, he went off up the Tump and he didn't come down again. It was generally thought that he'd gone off to join the New Model Army. He was never seen again around here, anyway, and the parishioners got on with their—er—activities in peace. Although, oddly enough, it seems that they never danced round the Tump again, on St John's Eve or any other Eve.'

PC Oliver opened his mouth to say that he had heard nonsense in his time but that . . . when he heard his superior give a curious grunt, as if he had been punched in the stomach. This was followed by a word he had never in his life heard Sergeant Prendergast utter. The word was: 'Marm.' It was accompanied by a good deal of gasping and creaking, and Oliver realised, to his amazement that his Sergeant was sinking down on one knee. He looked round. His first thought was that someone of the hippie persuasion had outflanked them, and got to the top of the Tump without their seeing her, and then he realised . . .

A woman stood at the top of the Tump above the kneeling Prendergast. She was bigger and shapelier than the women in Oliver's world normally were. Indeed she had that kind of hour-glass figure which hints (excitingly, if you like that kind of thing) at a kind of intricate interior scaffolding involving satin and whalebone, and lace, and *lacings* . . . Oliver firmly reined back his wandering thoughts from the direction in which they were heading. The woman's visible costume consisted of a full length white dress, of the kind which even PC Oliver knew was probably better described as a *gown* that left a lot of her shoulders and her splendid chest visible. She had long, bright hair, dressed in a number of thick plaits, each finished with a small golden apple. And the rain, which was still hurling itself in his face, was carefully avoiding her. She gave off a faint, silvery radiance . . . She was yet another of Sergeant Prendergast's supernatural acquaintance or he, PC Oliver was a lemon.

'You may rise, Sergeant,' she said.

Majestic, Oliver thought. That's what she is. She didn't precisely look like Queen Victoria, but Queen Victoria would have recognised her as a sister.

'Marm,' said the Sergeant, surging to his feet, 'I hope you will not consider us trespassers . . .'

'On the contrary,' the lady said, graciously. She bowed her head to the Sergeant, and the little golden apples tinkled together. 'You are most welcome. You are come to do Us a service.'

Are we, indeed? Oliver wondered.

'Anything that is within my power, and allowed by the rules of my Order,' Prendergast said. He sounded pretty sincere too.

'Oh, it is both,' said the lady firmly, 'I wish you to rescue the Reverend Jerningham from Us.'

'Ah,' said the Sergeant. 'I thought it might be something like that.'

'We took him into the hill many years ago, as you count such things . . .'

'Er—if I might be so bold as to *ask* marm, why did you take him?'

'He was upon Our territory between dusk and moon rising, and he was Our lawful prey. I thought to terrify him a little, and then he would be rescued, and loosed, chastened and humbled back to the world of mortals. But none came to his rescue,' she finished bitterly.

'M'm. I rather get the impression, marm, that no one wanted him back. The villagers even stopped their Midsummer dancing, in case someone rescued him by accident,' the Sergeant said heavily.

'And he has been preaching at us for three hundred years, Sergeant. He has ruined our revels and blighted our dances,' she cleared her throat slightly and straightened her shoulders, 'Wherefore the moon, the governess of the floods . . .'

'Yes marm, we understand . . .'

'Pale in her anger washes all the skies,' the lady continued grimly.

'Shocking,' Sergeant Prendergast agreed, 'but . . .'

'The mine men's morris is filled up with mud . . .'

'If you could tell us how to go about it . . .' he said.

'Of course. At sunrise my people will issue from the mound to perform our Midsummer Dance, as we must, though for too long we have done it without joy. He will be dancing with us—most reluctantly—and all you need do is to take him by the hand and draw him away from the dance . . .'

'I hope you're listening to this, Oliver,' the Sergeant said.

'But . . .' Oliver began. Then he closed his mouth. Of course he was going to be the one to do it. There was no point in arguing. Anyway it sounded straightforward enough.

'And, of course,' the lady was starting to sound just a little shifty, 'you'll have to—er—hang on to him. He may—er—*transform* a bit.'

'What!'

'Just pay attention to the lady,' said his Sergeant.

'But,' the lady swept on, 'provided you hold on to him, and *don't let him go* everything should be fine.'

'Got that, Oliver,' the Sergeant asked

cheerfully.

'Transform, transform into what . . .'

'The sun is rising,' said the lady.

'You could have fooled me,' Oliver muttered. He could see no difference in the black and rainy sky . . . but there was an abrupt change in the Tump. Suddenly they were no longer standing on a low grassy hill, but on the grass roof of a small building raised up on pillars. Light glowed from it, and a stream of depressed looking, grey-clad dancers emerged, hand-in-hand.

'Now, lad!' Sergeant Prendergast exclaimed. He gave Oliver a solid push between the shoulder blades which sent him skidding downwards again. He landed amongst the dancers, spitting out mud and grass again, and looked round for his prey. Actually the Reverend Jerningham was quite unmistakeable. He was wearing the tall hat and the broad white collar which PC Oliver recognised as the Puritan uniform from Hammer films.

'Do it, lad,' the Sergeant yelled.

With supreme reluctance Oliver tackled the clergyman. As soon as he gripped his bony hand Mr Jerningham transformed into a large lion. PC Oliver heard the hoarse, unmistakeable sound which is a masculine scream. Moments later, as he grappled with the lion, he realised who was doing the screaming. It was he. Later, he was to feel slightly ashamed of his reaction, but at the time it seemed entirely reasonable. He and the lion rolled over and over. The sensible thing, PC Oliver realised, would have been to let go, but somehow—somehow he didn't. Instead he kept his initial grip on the hand—now a paw— and grasped the mane for good measure. The lion turned into a very large snake.

'Hang on, lad,' Prendergast shouted. 'Try calling out his name.'

Oliver felt his hands sliding from something that seemed to be made up entirely of muscle and scales. 'Thaddeus,' he shouted. 'Thaddeus Jerningham.'

The snake hissed like a boiling kettle. It sounded extremely annoyed.

'Er—Mr Jerningham—Mr Jerningham, please . . .'

'Hang on,' the sergeant yelled.

And PC Oliver was rolling over in the mud, juggling a burning coal between his naked palms. 'Aghghgh! Thaddeus—aghaghgh— Jerningham,' he shrieked. And, instinctively plunged his burning hands, and the coal, into the wet grass. There was a jet of steam, and Mr Jerningham rose up out of the ground. PC Oliver screamed again. Mr Jerningham was now stark naked.

He stood for a moment, surveying the landscape. The rain had stopped. The clouds were rolling away, revealing a rosy red sky . . . and on the horizon PC Oliver saw the vanguard of those people that his superior officer had described as 'of the hippie and pagan persuasion'. The Reverend Mr Jerningham saw them too. He saw ladies festooned with silver charms, wearing occult robes and waving wands. He glimpsed a couple of hippie ladies who had so far entered into the spirit of the Midsummer revels as to bare their chests to the summer rain.

'Jezebel,' he bellowed, 'Endor! Flagrant fornication and bold bawdry!' and he charged towards them roaring. They scattered, shrieking. One lady, glimpsing PC Oliver's uniform called 'Police!'

PC Oliver did not respond to her cry. He examined his hands, and noticed that they showed no trace of burns. In front of him the Midsummer morning festivities were growing more exciting by the moment: a group of wiccan ladies were attempting to form a Circle of Protection, an attempt undermined by one of their own number who had reverted to type under the stress of the moment, and was trying to hit the Reverend Jerningham with her wand, and addressing him as 'Filthy Beast.' He was assuring her that she was Anathema, until his attention was distracted by a group of Morris men approaching grimly in formation across the field. They had shouldered their sticks like muskets, and the pipe and tabor which accompanied them ceased to play *Bonnie Green Garters* and changed to the more martial *Swaggering Bony.* Clearly both the Reverend and the Morris Men had recognised an old enemy in each other and neither side was going to back away from confrontation ...

PC Oliver became aware that somewhere behind him there were unmistakeable sounds of revelry and he turned round to see what it was. The Lady, with Sergeant Prendergast behind her, gripping her waist, was leading an exuberant conga around the hill, followed by the other dancers, their grey garments shredding away like the rain clouds to be replaced by brilliant colours.

'Ai ai ai ai *conga,*' they chanted, kicking joyfully and regularly in time to an invisible, but excellent samba-band.

Oliver wondered, for a hopeful moment, if the Sergeant was going to be dancing there for the next three hundred years, but then he and the Lady disengaged themselves from the jolly throng and came over to him.

'Well done, lad,' said the Sergeant, unexpectedly.

The Lady smiled, and bent down a little to kiss Oliver on the forehead.

'There,' said his Sergeant, 'nothing luckier than a fairy kiss.'

'Surely,' Oliver said, 'there's nothing luckier than being kissed by such a fairy.'

The Lady smiled again and the Midsummer sun came out.

The chimaera's small soft voice stopped.

'Who was the Lady?' I asked. 'And why did she quote Shakespeare?'

'She was the Queen of Elphame,' said the chimaera, reverently. 'And I wouldn't be surprised if Shakespeare wasn't quoting *Her* when he wrote *A Midsummer Night's Dream.*'

'Tit's Tump,' I said. 'That would be Titania then?'

'That is one of Her titles,' said the Chimaera primly, 'of course, She knew Shakespeare well. He'd often danced with Her. People like Will can come and go in Elphame as they please. It's people like the Reverend Jerningham who have trouble.'

'What on earth happened to him?' I asked.

'He became a very famous television personality,' said the chimaera in a small, shocked voice. 'And serve him right.'

THE DEPARTURE

The long summer was at last coming to an end. The mornings were colder and darker, and leaves were beginning to yellow and crisp. And things were changing in my life too. It began with a jubilant message from my True Love. He had been silent for a while, and I had been, as ever, divided between the fear that he was lying ill and uncared for in some student hostel, and the fear that he was having much too jolly a time in that same hostel to concern himself with me. But it turned out that a well-known television company had seen some of his choicer footage on YouTube, and was seriously considering asking him to make it into a travel series (*The EXTREMELY Rough Guide* was its tentative title) and he had been waiting until the offer looked firm enough to tell me about it.

I had two pieces of good news myself, along with one that was perhaps not quite so good . . . the best was that an agent had accepted my novel. True, there was, she told me, a terrific amount of re-writing to do, but I was quite prepared for that. Interestingly, the reason she had been drawn to it was the ending 'It's so unusual to find a really nice, happy ending these days,' she had said. I told the chimaera, and it looked very smug.

The second was when I got a job with one of the major opera houses—not as a singer I hasten to say, but as one of the supporting actors. This meant ten weeks of steady and very welcome money—which was just as well perhaps, because the not-so-good news was that my landlord wanted my attic for a relative, and my occupancy (which had been fairly unofficial) was due to come to an end. A friend had very kindly offered me a room to stay in while I looked round and found somewhere for myself and my True Love to live, but I had not, I am afraid, told her about the chimaera. I had grown so fond of him that I hoped he would *not* dissipate, but I was not at all sure how I was going to explain him to my friend. Or even to my True Love when he came home . . .

On my last night in the attic I sat drinking lemon-balm tea amongst my neatly packed possessions, ready to leave in the morning, when my friend was going to collect me in a van belonging to a pizza company. I was half looking forward to the changes I was facing, and half concerned about the chimaera. It was drowsing on the sofa, and I went to the window to have a last look at the strange panorama of London that was visible from my high window. But a sound from the mews below caused me to look down. And I saw that the mews was full of people—and, indeed animals—and there was a police car too . . . two policeman, one fat and slovenly, one young and rather good looking were standing by the car—I recognised Sergeant Prendergast and PC Oliver at once. A very beautiful lady in a white gown was standing beside them, and near her was another beauty, this one in a Grecian dress, with a shining crescent moon in her hair, standing with her arm thrown over the neck of a stag, there was a huge red haired biker, and a slender leather clad biker lady (her helmet firmly in place, I was pleased to see), a nice looking couple holding hands with three small children and a tiny hairy man, all of whom were bouncing with excitement, and while I watched two frogs leaped onto the bonnet of the police car and stood on their back legs, waving at me. The handsome dwarf and his willow lady were there too, with a whole crowd of woodland creatures, while on the outskirts of the crowd I saw three fairly nondescript men who must have been Old Bob, Martin and the stage-struck devil because they were all carrying cardboard cups of coffee as if they had just been called from a coffee break on a film set. With them were two people who unmistakeably worked in a museum, a handsome man in an old fashioned military uniform—and a ravishing beautiful lady in a black lace ball dress and a great many rubies.

And they were all waving, and clapping, and cheering—I waved back, but a little sadly because I knew they must have come to say goodbye to the chimaera. I heard a small sound in the room and looked round quickly. But it was no longer on the sofa. And when I turned back the mews was empty and gleaming under a full moon.

'It was very kind of them all to come,' I said aloud, 'but I wish I had said goodbye to it myself . . .'

And a solid, furry form sprang onto the windowsill beside me. The chimaera had not dissipated. It had turned into a very handsome white cat. I caught it in my arms and it rubbed its nose against mine.

'How lovely,' I said. 'You are even more beautiful now, and I shall have no trouble about introducing you to my friend. But I shall miss your stories.'

The chimaera smiled a cat smile. 'But I have lots more stories,' it said. 'Many of them, of course, about cats.'

I nearly dropped it. 'You can still talk!'

'All cats can talk,' it said, with a faint air of contempt. 'But they don't usually tell other people about it . . . but seeing that you're a friend . . .'

'How wonderful . . .'

'I do like a happy ending,' it said.

And so do I.